Kiss Me Once Again

Also by Gail Kittleson

Women of the Heartland Series

In Times Like These
With Each New Dawn
A Purpose True

and

In This Together
Catching Up With Daylight

Kiss Me Once Again

A Women of the Heartland Story

Gail Kittleson

WordCrafts

Dedicated to all the women who sacrificed so much.

Chapter One

"Anybody here?"

Glenora replaced a bolt before digging her heels into the floor to coax her mechanic's dolly from the bottom side of a '37 Chevy truck. When the garage's bare light bulb glared in her eyes, Slim Anderson stared down at her.

"Ah, there you are. Knew your dad wouldn't leave the shop unattended."

Glenora pulled a rag from her back overall pocket and wiped a gooey grease patch from her cheek. Unattended? Oh, no! Never the shop. Maybe her hair, her clothes, even her heart, but never this busy garage, the only one in Halberton, Iowa.

Slim held out his hand and pulled her to eye level. Glenora shook out her arms and the kinks in her back. "Whew—this old rattletrap's seen better days, I'd say. Been under there an hour, but it seems like I just got started."

"Delivering eggs takes a toll on trucks, that's for sure. Harm can't just not show up—those housewives'd have his hide if he messed with their egg money." Slim gave her a minute to orient to the upright world. "Your daddy around today?"

"He's taking a part over to Benson." She waved a hand

toward the back of the brick building, where line after line of partially rusted vehicles filled the pasture separating the garage from their house. "Somebody needed a starter for a... Anyway, he said he'll be back before noon."

Slim fingered a grimy mechanism in his big brown farmer hand.

"I'm guessing that came from your Allis Chalmers?"

"Right, a Model RC." Slim paused for effect, but Glenora had heard it all before, how he'd saved to purchase the orange tractor when it came out in '39, and how putting the engine of the Model B on the chassis of the larger model WC had birthed the amazing machine. Not to mention how well the trusty tractor had served him until...

"Somethin's haywire with the gearshift. Took the blamed thing off to check on a squeak, but after I greased everything to kingdom come and went to put it back together..."

Glenora took the small iron piece from him and turned it over. "I know what you mean, but I've never seen this piece before. Sorry."

"That's all right. A fella can't know everything these days." Slim's already sunburned face reddened. "I mean a *gal*..."

Glenora's chuckle eased the lines in his forehead. "It's all right. Daddy'll know. Maybe he can drive out to your place later this afternoon. I'm sure you're anxious to get your crops in."

"Yeah." Slim glanced around the shop, twitching his nose at the mélange of odors. "Betcha it sure helps, you takin' care of everything around here when your dad's gone."

"As much as I can. Red would have recognized this piece too, I'm sure he would."

"That boy's always been a smart one." Slim slid his stained

hat back from his receding hairline. "Can't help but wonder how all our fellas are doin' over there."

The backs of Glenora's eyes burned to think of her tender-hearted little brother at war. With almost four years between them, Red became her charge when Mama got sick, and his fear of losing Mama had torn him apart. How many nights had he run to Glenora for comfort?

And then the worst happened—overnight, Mama faded away. A raw wave washed Glenora's throat as she stared across the street through the big filthy garage window. Halberton's morning traffic crawled bug-like down the main two-lane concourse. Right now, the flow consisted of an old green farm truck and a boy lucky enough to own a bicycle...and the mountain of dust they raised.

"We keep believin' they're all right, don't we—our Sam and your Red?" Slim studied the Red Cross office, too. The full-length window boasted several posters—in one, a wild-haired girl in a navy-blue sailor shirt grinned out at the world. Glenora had memorized the words marching beside the portrait, "Gee, I wish I were a man. I'd join the Navy."

The entreaty at the bottom stuck with her, too. "Be a man and do it. United States Navy Recruiting Station." The appeal worked—Red and nearly every other eligible young man in Mitchell County had done it—joined up, endured boot camp, and shipped out long ago.

"Our Sam couldn't take his eyes off them posters his last year of high school. Still wake up in the morning when our cranky old rooster crows and can hardly believe he's gone."

"I know what you mean. I thought Daddy'd never recover when Red enlisted. Still, he signed the papers that let him go before he turned eighteen."

"'Course. Just like me. What choice did we have?" Slim gave a massive sigh. "Gotta save the world from the Japs... and then there's Joe Lundene. Been three years already since he went down at Pearl Harbor."

Slim seemed to have no intention of leaving soon, but Glenora could think of plenty of topics she'd rather discuss. Slim cocked his jaw to the side, which signaled he was about to meddle in someone's business.

Preparing herself for whatever gossip would emerge, Glenora decided to slip back under the egg truck. *I swanny, these older men go on and on—maybe even more than the ladies in the church kitchen.*

Just as she opened her mouth to tell Slim he needn't squat down, she could hear fine from underneath the vehicle, a screech from the back door saved her. It wasn't that she'd put Joe out of her mind, if that were possible—but she'd far rather keep her thoughts about him to herself. The mention of the Pearl Harbor attack still caused something in her to shrivel.

Joe, her high school beau, had been so proud of the Arizona. Being on that ship meant the world to him. Just yesterday, she'd finally tucked his last letter into the shoebox where she kept the rest. Thirty of them altogether, in his easy-to-read penmanship. He'd taken his English classes seriously and intended to become a history teacher someday.

For the life of her, she couldn't see what good talking about that horrible attack did, but people seemed incapable of leaving it alone. Maybe because Joe was the first from town to give his life for the cause, they clung to the catastrophe. She supposed folks like Slim would still be chattering about Joe twenty years from now, but she focused on moving through each day and taking the memories that still inundated her one at a time.

The back door hinges whined again, and thankful for this reprieve, Glenora left Slim to study the metal piece he'd brought in. With singular intent, she scuttled across the dirt floor toward the back of the garage and caught her dad's eye.

"Glad you're home early, Dad. Slim's out front with a tractor part I don't recognize. I'll run home and make us some lunch." She slunk out the back way beyond the garbage barrels and made her way down the first line of rusting old trucks and cars in the otherwise empty lot.

The roof of their house showed through a pleasant grove of tall pines that blocked this half-acre from view—good to have a destination. Around her, birdsong and rustlings in the overgrown grass reminded her life still existed outside the garage, where she'd spent far too much time the past few months. She breathed deep of early summer—lilacs and honeysuckle still in the air. Soon enough, August would descend with its humidity.

But halfway down the row of cast-off cars, the thought of Joe perishing in those murky Pacific waters overcame her. She slid down the fender of a 1929 Model L-29 black Cord and leaned back into its solid warm metal. A few weeks earlier, she'd overheard Slim and Dad talking about her.

"She doin' all right 'bout Joe n' everything?"

Probably Joe, handsome and as friendly as apple pie, would've found some other girl, pretty and petite, if he'd come back from the war. He showed her attention back in high school, but until he kissed her on their junior prom night, she thought he was just being nice to a lanky, awkward girl who hadn't yet grown into her own body. His lips barely brushed hers, but she'd never forget that moment.

Joe knew full well she was almost two years older than him, having started school late and then losing a year to a bout with scarlet fever. He couldn't miss the mass of freckles speckling her nose and outstanding cheekbones, and also knew that no boys were lined up to ask her out—with less than a hundred students in the whole high school, everyone knew.

She closed her eyes and clasped the locket Joe gave her later that summer after they watched the fireworks display down by the river. He'd walked her out back in their yard, and under the rose trellis, gave her their first real kiss. The tingle of his touch still burned Glenora's lips. She'd just turned nineteen the week before, and believed she'd never experience anything like this.

"I know we're young, but my mind's made up, Glen. You're the one for me."

Looking into her eyes, Joe pulled out the locket with his picture inside. "With all the war talk, we can't know what the future will bring, but this'll remind you that you're my girl, in case you ever forget."

By that fall when he entered boot camp, Mama lay in her grave. And when some Iowa boys got called up early for duty in the Pacific, Joe was among them. No high school graduation...no senior prom.

Then came Pearl Harbor. Even though final word had been slow in coming, she'd known Joe had perished. But she went through the motions at school and took Mama's place at home. Then, in February, Red signed up, too.

When the Principal notified her that Iowa State University

had given her a scholarship, she could hardly rejoice. With Dad alone in the shop, how could she leave? He needed help, so of course, she plunged in right after graduation.

As for romance, she figured she'd had her chance. In a recessed corner of her heart, she sealed that compartment and marked it O-V-E-R.

Sunshine on the dilapidated Cord warmed her through, and Glenora shook herself back into the present. Better race home to make those sandwiches. She leaped over a straggly fence and up the three back porch steps. Inside the kitchen, she opened the Frigidaire and slapped together a quick meal. As on every other weekday, she carried the food to the garage in a brown paper bag, along with a quart jar of water from the kitchen pump.

Just in time to hear a snitch of conversation between Dad and Slim...he was *still* here? She paused on the threshold. "Got our nephew comin' out t' the farm, Roy. Back from the fight, wounded in the face and leg and spent the last few weeks convalescin' out t' Walter Reed, but now they're releasin' him."

Dad scraped something along the cement, so Glenora lost some of Slim's words. "...smart guy—always wanted to go into engineering. Wish he'd take advantage of the GI Bill n' go down to Iowa State."

"Makes sense." Whatever it was Dad dragged, he timed it just right to block the first part of Slim's reply, but not the rest.

"She still sweet on Joe Lundene?"

"Glenora keeps her thoughts to herself, like her mother. Strong women. Just wish Eleanore hadn't caught that awful flu bug."

"Yeah, tough times for you. Well, we might could use some help getting Hank back on his feet. You don't s'pose..."

Glenora cleared her throat and banged the door open. Dad fiddled over Slim's broken tractor part as Slim backed toward the front door, still jabbering away. "Prob'ly brought this on myself, Roy, tryin' t' fix that squeak, but a man's gotta try, doncha know? 'Sides, you ain't never failed me yet."

"Nope."

For some time, the sign above the shop had needed repair. That was an understatement. Anybody driving down Main looking for *Carson Garage* would have a tough time. A violent May rainstorm had brought down a massive hard maple that narrowly missed the window. In mid-July sun, a jagged mark still curved right through the *r* in *Carson*. Arms akimbo, Glenora stared up at the open wound on her return trip from the post office.

"Maybe if I climbed up there and..." She opened the door, but turned when boot steps approached.

"Miss Carson?"

A giant of a man peered at her from at least ten inches above. She'd grown used to looking down at folks, but this fellow towered a full head beyond her five-feet-eleven, maybe more, and looked as though he could lift a tree by the roots if he had a mind to.

"Yes?"

He held out his hand, a worker's hand, tough and muscled thick. His deep tan highlighted a slash across his left cheekbone, with white stitch marks embedded in the grown-over skin. The gouge meandered up between the bluest eyes she'd ever seen, before finding a home in the middle of his forehead.

"You may not remem..." He blinked and started over. "I'm

Hank McCarthy. I knew your older brother Tom years ago."

Try as she might, Glenora failed to dredge up a memory. "I'm sorry, I don't recall..."

"I wouldn't expect you to... I only came to my aunt and uncle's for a month in the summer, but me and Tom got to know each other pretty well."

Glenora looked away. The last thing he needed was someone staring at his scar. Then it came to her—this must be Slim and Minnie Anderson's nephew. Dad mentioned something about Slim's sister having trouble—the kind of trouble you only referred to, never described in full.

"She's always been fidgety and flighty, doncha know, even as a little girl. But this—guess the doctor's got a mind to send her down t' Independence for a spell." The name of that town, somewhere around Waterloo, always brought a shudder with it, since the state mental institution was there.

Something niggled at the back of Glenora's mind, and she glanced up at this man's raw, but kindly face. "Oh, wait—I think I do remember something—you and Tom went fishing a lot?"

Hank nodded. "That's right." He turned his farmer cap in fingers the size of the long johns Lucille Fletcher sold to Olsen's Café.

"Tom left years ago to work for Hormel up in Austin, but he'd remember you, for sure. How can I help you?"

"Your father, ma'am—is he inside?"

Being called ma'am seemed peculiar, but Dad's whistle from the shop reminded Glenora of her manners. "Yes. He's finished with your uncle's tractor part. Go right on in."

The ramshackle door creaked open to a flood of thick greasy dust, tire rubber, and that nameless underlying scent

Glenora attributed to the town stable being here for so many decades before Dad bought the place twenty years ago. Hank followed her, and she noticed he shut the door without a bang—not easy with its broken springs.

Dad peeked out from under a Studebaker's hood. "Hello there, Hank. Welcome to the center of Halberton."

Hank 's stiff bearing relaxed a bit as Dad waved him over. "Hear you've got some experience with engines. Would you mind taking a look under here, son?"

Soon, the two of them mulled over the motor. Glad to be out from under the hood herself, Glenora took the chance to work on the accounts. So Hank might work here? She wished Dad had given her fair warning, but then, when did he ever?

And heaven knew, they needed help. Even with gas rationing and the new speed limit, a never-ending stream of folks still required repairs. For one thing, the need for food for the troops had farmers increasing their production, which meant more tractor and truck breakdowns.

An ever-growing list of customers with broken items listed beside their names occupied the counter, front and center. Every morning, Dad shook his head over it. "Don't see how we can whittle this down much today—gotta get finished with what we've already started."

Accounts receivable showed seventeen unpaid jobs, plus all the ones Dad neglected to write down—if only people brought in their payments as promptly as they expected him to answer their pleas for help. He met himself coming and going, but already today, several men complained about how long they'd had to wait.

As usual, he calmed them down. "I'll get to you soon's I can." He gestured to the five motors forming a pentagon on his left. "Got your engine lined up right over there, but fair's fair."

By late morning, a gaggle of customers, in addition to some who'd come in for the news, gathered in one corner. On this sunny July day, the temperature rose by the minute, so they sought the shop's cool brick interior, just as they gathered around the pot-bellied stove during the winter months.

"Can't believe we're still breakin' through them Normandy hedgerows."

"But didja hear? Last night they said our boys captured St. Lo, and Saipan fell, too. More 'n twenty-five thousand Japs killed. We're on the win, fellas."

"Our bombers made the diff'rence. Them air strikes done it for us in France. I'm figurin' Al Hanson's son mighta prob'ly been in on that one. Flies across the channel regular-like."

Glenora wrote *troops took St. Lo* under July 18 on the wall calendar behind the counter. Even if she happened to miss a war report in the evenings, somebody would carry the latest in the next day.

Under the running board of a Studebaker, Hank's huge boots stuck out a foot farther than Dad's, so she took care to skirt them en route to the back door. Intermittent clinks, clunks, and exclamations provided certainty that the two of them would work out this mechanical puzzle in due time.

With so many men lounging in the corner, Glenora thought it safe to take a walk. One of them could deal with any customers for ten minutes. She'd been working since six this morning, and her head had started to throb. She headed west, hungry for the comfort of the river road. Maybe it was because Dad used to let her tag along when he took Tom fishing, but something about the rise of low bushes in the ditch and majestic oaks along the bank soothed her.

In the distance, the water eddied in a slow summertime swoosh over the manmade dam. Bill Behr still ran the old sawmill, especially now that the Navy sought so many ship-building materials. Once a month he sent a load to Chicago, and from August through October, added bales of hemp the farmers grew for ropes.

Dad used to tell how he helped men cut great blocks of ice at the pond that pooled down the hill, and dragged them on sledges up to the grocery store's warehouse, and how those blocks stayed cool in their shady sawdust beds to serve the townspeople's coolers in the heat of summer. Seemed impossible they could last so long.

The last time she walked down here, dry oak leaves still clung to otherwise bare branches, though it was almost budding time. Funny how certain leaves clung on through the winter, brown and crisp right up until the new spring buds leafed out.

Today, though, all shone dappled green and radiant—honeysuckle bushes spawned into trees, wild lilacs still spread their scent, and cottonwoods wafted white fluff to a carefree breeze. As she breathed in the freshness, Iowa's midsummer beauty refreshed Glenora in spite of the heat.

Nature still carried on, regardless of demanding customers and in spite of the war. Even this brief respite calmed her fears about Red and life in general. Strengthened for the long afternoon ahead, she retraced her steps back to the garage.

Chapter Two

One late August day when Glenora came back from making sandwiches for the men, some children ranged through the weeds along the back of the shop. One especially chubby-cheeked little girl with two front teeth missing accosted her at the entrance to the vehicle lot.

"Mith Carthon, my mommy thaid to ask your 'mithon to pick milkweeds out here."

A boy whose enormous brown eyes testified to a family connection sidled up beside his little sister. "She means *permission*. We gotta gather milkweed, cause the soldiers need life vests, 'specially them Navy fellas."

"Why, of course. Pick every single one."

Glenora set down her packet and walked the children into the weedy yard.

"Did you know my brother joined the Navy?"

"He did?" The boy's eyes popped. " Wow—I'm gonna join up, too, soon's I can."

"I hope the war ends before then so you won't have to. And I hope you find thousands of pods out here, maybe even millions. Just think, you may help save some sailor's life."

Two serious children nodded in tandem.

"Oh, and do be careful out there, there might be some rusty pieces sticking out to trip you."

The boy put his hand protectively on his sister's shoulder, and they skipped off. That child's dress was about two sizes too small—why, in less than an hour, she could stitch up a new one for her.

With a sigh, Glenora turned toward the garage. "But they're Joneses, I'm pretty sure, and their mom would never accept a gift like that."

This afternoon, the two would be back with some scrap metal they'd found somewhere, for the war drive—the fighting affected even these little tykes. She picked up the sandwiches without noticing Hank over by the burn barrel until he strode over.

"Oh, Hank...here's your lunch."

"Thanks. Mind if I eat out here?"

"No, go ahead. Good idea to get out of the shop for a while." She divvied out his share and walked in on Slim having a chat with Dad at the counter. Ever since that first day Hank worked on the Studebaker, she'd brought sandwiches along for him, too. The long hours he put in made all the difference for Dad, and for her, too. Finally, she'd caught up on the books and created a filing system.

Things went along fine, except for Slim stopping in every few days with his endless hints. Today was no different. "I see there's a new movie at the theatre. You young folks oughta take it in."

Now Glenora understood—Hank had sought more than fresh air out back. When Slim came around, Hank tended to his work with such intensity, he might have been deaf. Glenora understood, and had to suppress the urge to tell Slim to lay off.

She set the sandwich packet down. "Here's your food, Dad. Mr. Anderson, could I talk with you while Dad eats?"

Slim raised his bushy eyebrows, as if nothing could be more important than bothering Dad. But he followed her out to the front.

"I've got a question for you, if you don't mind." Leaving the door open, she drew him further as Dad threw her a grateful look. "Have you noticed the big rip in this sign? How would you go about fixing it?"

He rubbed his chin. "Why, your Dad knows, 'a course."

"That's just the thing, Slim. He doesn't even have time to notice. You can see he's busy from dawn 'til dusk. So I thought maybe I'd take on this project myself and surprise him."

"Let me think on it. Made outta steel, ain't it? Maybe I've got somethin' out at the farm you could paint up real nice. And Hank could help you."

She ought to have known.

"My wife'd fix you two a good dinner, and our creek's so pretty this time of year..."

Manners forgotten, Glenora turned to go inside and shut the door behind her.

The afternoon passed with two jobs completed and four more added to the list. Before going home for the day, she called out a reminder. "Dad, don't forget the meeting tonight at church—remember, the board is deciding what to do about the roof."

His lack of response made her grin. He'd be the first to volunteer for the job, but detested the ordered process of discussion, voting, and delegating responsibilities. Aware that he knew she still waited for his answer, she stalled half a minute more. His answer sounded even more distant than normal.

"If you don't see me by seven, better stop over. We're just about to get this one figured out, Glen."

Mama called her Nora except on rare occasions when something irritated her. But as long as she could remember, Dad had called her Glen. And so had Joe.

Daddy calls me Glen and you call me Nora. Mama, why'd you name me Glenora?

Because, dear, your father was absolutely convinced you'd be a boy.

So I disappointed him?

No, but we'd waited so long for a baby after Tommy—eight years. We almost gave up, but your Daddy had his heart set on a brother for Tom. He adjusted real quick, though. Two blinks of your big brown eyes won his heart.

And then, unexpectedly, Red had come along three years later, one of those nice surprises in life, Mama always said. Glenora recalled her new baby brother's rosy tint, and Tom exclaiming, "Good grief, he's all red—do all babies look like this?"

Strangely, *Red* stuck, even with such a dignified given name: Victor Albert Carson. That name appeared on official papers three times that Glenora remembered— Red's confirmation certificate, his diploma, and his draft registration.

On the way to make supper, she stopped at the garden to pick a ripe tomato and some string beans. Late afternoon sun dipped behind the wooden fence bordering the back yard, bringing Red to mind again. How many times had she watched him crawl over that edifice, late for a meal? And the sunset reminded her of Joe, too, devouring a watermelon out here on a late summer evening.

This back yard held so many tender memories. Thanks to Hank helping Dad, she'd at least had time to hoe the garden before the worst of the oppressive humidity set in. Hoeing did her good—something to tend besides grouchy people.

And now, the steady stream of produce began—peas and beans, tomatoes, onions, radishes, strawberries, and raspberries. Later would come squash, bushels of apples from Mama's favorite tree, and the raspberries' second crop. The petunias Mama planted years ago showed up faithfully year after year, along with tulips, peonies, daylilies, and cheery yellow daisies that floated on long stems like a sea of butterflies.

This year, she'd hardly had time to weed them, or to deadhead, but she'd get to it. The luxury of time to work alone out here with no interruptions, no whiners or complainers, and above all, no one spouting last evening's war news almost made Glenora dizzy.

Mama spent so many hours nurturing her plant babies—no wonder she loved this space so much. Red became her number one helper as soon as he could walk. Back then, he declared he wanted to become a farmer, but once he started following Dad around the garage, his ideas of the future transformed. He'd be a mechanic, of course. Hopefully he still could.

Finally she pulled herself inside to slice the beef roast she'd cooked yesterday. She fried leftover potatoes, cooked some string beans and set the table, but realized at six-fifty that Dad needed a reminder.

In fading light, she trekked back to the garage, let herself in the back, and moved through a shadowy jungle of boxes, tractor tires, fenders, and barrels full of parts. But when she entered the main section, her heart stopped at the scene before her. Dad sat stooped over on a chair with Hank down on one knee, looking up into his face.

In an instant, the change struck her—why hadn't she noticed how Dad's shoulders shrank around his chest? His breath came hard, and his skin glinted pale as milkweed fluff.

His rasp sickened her. She grabbed the door to steady herself. Hank must've heard, and jerked his head her way. He always seemed in control, but now he opened his mouth to no avail.

Glenora raced over and touched Dad's shoulder. "What is it?"

Clearly, he couldn't reply, so she turned to Hank. The torn expression on his face sent a sharp pain through her gut.

"Hank, please."

"He... his br... breathing got like this about ten minutes a... ago. I got him to sit down. May... maybe it'll calm down."

"Yes." Glenora's pulse sprinted as wildly as her thoughts. "You did the right thing. I'm so glad you're here. I'll run and get Doc Ayers. Keep Dad quiet, okay?"

Hank focused on her for a moment, and a shadow passed through his eyes. Then he inhaled as if he'd never breathed before and took Dad's hand.

"Roy, did you hear that? Doc'll be here right away. I'll wait right here with you."

"Blamed if that old coot didn't..."

"Didn't what?" Doc strode into the room with a notepad in his hand. "Do exactly what I knew you didn't want me to? Yes, that's right, Roy. I brought you straight here, because I thought you might not make it otherwise."

Already pale, Dad blanched even whiter.

"A time like this comes for all of us, and you're no exception.

You've got to slow down, Roy. I see the shop light on at six in the morning and late into the evening. Our bodies weren't made to work without enough rest." Doc tapped his finger on Roy's chest. "Your old ticker needs rest."

Roy leaned back into his hospital pillow. His lopsided frown reminded Glenora of their old hound dog languishing in the porch shade on a summer afternoon. Stymied by Doc, his old buddy, he could find no adequate retort.

"What do you say—can you take it a little easier?"

"I say get me out of here. Can't believe you brought me in the ambulance."

"Well, your condition scared me." Doc clipped some notes to the foot of the bed and stood there a little longer. "I'm tellin' you, Roy. You've got to ease up."

He gave Glenora a knowing look and left the room. His heels clicked down the hall like warning beeps. Glenora kneaded her upper lip with her teeth. Obviously, Doc seemed to think she held some sway here, but what did he know?

Silent until now, Hank rose from the corner and pulled his chair close to the bed. "Mr. Carson, I can work more hours."

At his simple statement, a change came over her dad. The tight lines around his mouth loosened, and his fisted right hand went slack. Hank slipped his forearm under Dad's shoulders and helped him sit up a bit more.

"That better?"

"Yeah." Roy turned to Glenora. "But I ain't stayin' here all night, and that's the end of it."

Focused solely on their patient, Hank suddenly seemed the have developed the gift of gab, and without any stuttering. "You're already here—makes sense to stay at least 'til morning, don't you think, Mr. Carson?"

Roy closed his eyes as if to gather strength. "Call me Roy, will ya?" Hank nodded. A full minute passed as Roy stared at the wall. Then he quietly repeated his question.

"Yeah, I s'pose."

"Do you need anything else tonight? Just say the word and I'll get it for you."

Glenora leaned back in her chair. A great weight shifted from her shoulders—clearly, Hank was taking things in hand. Her dad, docile as a kitten, shook his head as if he'd never been more content.

"Do you think you can sleep now, or you want us to stay a while longer?"

"It'd help if you'd turn out that confounded light up there." Dad's irritated tone belied the way he relaxed against his pillow.

Hank scrambled to the switch, and the bare bulb gradually gave up its power. For a man who'd taken no initiative but to follow her dad's orders at the shop, he seemed to have undergone an alteration, too.

Good thing, because weakness suddenly sheathed Glenora like an August heat wave. The walk home loomed impossible.

"Well then, Mr. Car... Roy. I expect we ought to get home so we can open the garage early in the morning and get a head start on the day's work. Don't worry about a thing. Your daughter's got things covered up front, and I'll do everything I can to help her out."

When he stood, Glenora followed suit. Shadowing Hank never occurred to her before, but at this moment, following his lead seemed mighty good.

She leaned over her dad and kissed his forehead. "Good night then, Daddy. I hope you sleep well. See you in the morning."

"About that—I ain't stayin' here long."

"No. I'll be over and find out when Doc says you can leave."

His sour look gave her pause, but Hank reached over and shook his hand. "We'll get you home as soon as we can."

Outside Doc's house, Glenora tripped on the bottom step and Hank caught her by the elbow. "You all right to walk home?" He waited until she steadied herself. "I can run back to the garage and get my car if you want me to."

"Oh, thank you, but the fresh air will do me good."

"You're sure?"

"Yes."

"Do you mind if I walk with you?"

"Oh, no—please do. But I'd think you'd be worn out after sprinting over here."

"I'm used to..." He shrugged. "Moving around a lot."

An image of Hank slinking through enemy territory ran through Glenora's mind. For such a large man, he moved like a lynx. She realized she didn't even know where he had served.

Behind them, twilight coated the windows, draped for the blackout. The big old white house wasn't exactly a hospital, but Dad sure thought so, and Doc must have had a good reason for not driving him to the real thing in Osage. Had he really thought Roy might die? Glenora wished she'd have asked him a few questions.

The blackout shades over the high windows created a pleasant ambience, as though candles instead of light bulbs burned in the rooms. With every step, cool air calmed Glenora, and gratitude overwhelmed her.

"I really don't know what to say, Hank. What a shock—Dad's

hardly been sick a day in his life. I can't thank you enough for what you did in there, and at the shop."

"Your dad's done a lot for me."

His quiet presence and her exhaustion turned the six-block walk into a mellow interlude. Thankfully, Hank seemed not to mind the silence. Approaching the front door of the shop, he took charge as though he sensed she could barely take another step.

"Sit here on the bench while I lock up, all right? Then I'll walk you home."

With no inclination to argue. Glenora complied. When Hank emerged, he took her elbow and guided her the front way home. It'd been ages since she followed the path past the Collier's house and the vine-covered picket fence surrounding their lush garden. From his doghouse, Teddy gave a single bark, reminding the world he was on the alert.

Sweet heady scents hung over her mother's weedy flower-bed and up to the front gate Glenora used to swing on as a child. From Mrs. Mosely's front yard came the creak, creak of her front porch swing—out enjoying the summer evening.

Home—what the boys over there are fighting for—what Hank fought for.

As if he lived here, Hank opened the gate and stood back to let Glenora pass. At the break in the sidewalk, he leaned toward her a little. "Front or back?" She gestured toward the back.

He preceded her up the porch steps, opened the door, and tipped his cap. "Sleep late if you can, ma'am. I'll be there early to take care of things."

Halfway through the doorway, Glenora grasped his arm, and his steadiness chimed a bell deep within her. "Hank, thank you so much."

"Umm." He turned to go, but she hung on.

"I... you're calling Dad Roy, so would you mind calling me Glenora?"

Long shadows almost hid Hank's scar, and she noticed a bump two-thirds of the way up his nose. He gave a slight nod. "If you want me to."

"I do. Yes."

"All right. You'll go right to bed?"

"I will."

"Good."

And then, without a sound, he was gone. He must hold tight control over every muscle. Glenora listened a while longer, but not the slightest rustle resonated, not even when Hank opened and closed the gate. Or maybe he simply stepped over. Cricket chirps and cicadas owned the night, and the haze over the garden created a wonderland of circling fireflies.

They reminded Glenora of the string beans—she'd better keep close watch on them, and the zucchini and tomatoes could be ready overnight, too. If only she had more time to spend out here—how would she ever manage to do all the canning before the first hard frost?

She'd have to worry about that another day, but for now, Dad simply had to get better. Locking the door behind her, she crossed the porch into the kitchen and leaned against the cool plaster wall. The room's familiar shadows whispered what they had several times during the past few years. After what happened tonight, things might never be the same again.

Chapter Three

This early September morning when Glenora left the house, a thick frost bronzed the world around her. Gold and orange leaves dappled clear robin's-egg blue sky, and every shingle on the carriage house roof glinted white in the sunshine. Her sigh launched into the welcome coolness.

Yesterday she canned the last of the beans and dragged the potatoes down to the fruit cellar, the whole while hearing Mama declare that she shouldn't be working on Sunday. But the weatherman forecasted a hard frost, so there wasn't much choice but to work straight through after coming home from church.

The garden still held so much promise, so Dad covered the tomatoes and beans with a heavy canvas at dusk. Mixed emotions overwhelmed Glenora—twenty-nine quarts of beans wouldn't hold them over the winter, true, but she cringed at the thought of heating up the canner again some evening this week after an already long day at the garage.

If only Mama... She shuddered going up the back steps—lamenting her death was such a waste of time and energy. She'd give Dad about one more day—maybe half a day—to follow Doc's orders. For him, being housebound included the back yard, where he'd picked up bushels of black walnuts during the past week.

She warned him when she saw him stripping the pea vines and piling them in the burn pile. "Too much leaning over for you—you already picked up walnuts today. Remember what Doc said, Dad. I'll get to cleaning out the garden one of these days—won't take me long."

His dark look encouraged her, because it revealed how his color had returned the past couple of days, along with his feisty spirit. Seeing him so pale in that hospital bed really had given her a turn. And he'd been "good" for nearly a week now, working only from noon until six. But tomorrow, she guessed, he'd pronounce himself healed and don his grimy overalls for a full day's work.

She strode through the yard toward the back quarter of their property between the garage and house, pausing near a post where Dad had set an odd-shaped squash he'd picked. Morning sunlight emphasized the vegetable's bizarre angles and brought Glenora a chuckle.

"Wonder if he thought this looked a little like me?"

Long ago, she'd accepted the lay of her facial bones, seemingly at odds with each other. Once, on a shopping trip with Aunt Henrietta, Dad's sister, she'd learned a trick that seemed natural enough. "Be sure you wear clothes with interest at the neck, dear. Shirtwaists with a sweater draw the eye downward."

Away from my face, you mean. Aunt Henrietta meant well, and often accompanied her helpful advice with references to how much she looked like Glenora. Instead of a bare-shouldered prom dress, she'd found one whose sleeves angled up in classic stitching that tied at the neck. She held it up to herself.

"See how this streamlines me from the elbows up? Makes my long arms look a little more normal, don't you think?"

In the end, that was the dress Glenora chose, and she had to admit, wearing it made her feel elegant. For a moment, she allowed memories from prom night to hold sway.

"Well, that dress must've worked for Joe." She set the peculiar squash down. There. She'd finally said his name out loud. It was about time, since her images of him had decreased even more lately. Must be all the work this summer.

She plunged across dry grass that needed mowing onto the hardened path through the pasture. Voices drifted from Minor and Effie Peterson's back yard. They and other neighbors had brought over enough produce for a month during the past week, and Glenora had shared some of everything with Hank.

At noon yesterday, he finished off some fried chicken, scalloped corn, and the last three pieces of a chocolate cake she whipped up on Saturday night. She ate her share, too, and enjoyed seeing someone enjoy a meal so much.

Perched on a solid metal stool pulled up to the counter, Hank offered more details about his private life than he had in the entire time he'd worked here. "I'm moving into a room in town tonight. My uncle and aunt won't like it, but it's time for me to be on my own again."

Stunned into silence at this admission, Glenora only nodded. But as Hank removed his overalls before leaving, she managed a comment. "I hope Slim doesn't get upset when you tell him."

Hank shrugged. "Oh, he will, but I've made up my mind. I appreciate all they've done for me, but I'm no longer the kid who used to stay with them in the summer. Slim will keep on popping in here to say I need some fun in my life. He's told me that so many times, he must think I'm deaf."

Glenora chuckled and shook her head. "He keeps saying that to me, too. Says I need to enjoy life a little more—*all work and no play*, you know. But with Red still over there, and Dad recovering, I..."

"Yeah, I know. But Slim's relentless, and I've had all I can take. Besides, I figure it'll add another half hour to the work day if I live right here in town."

"I'm almost sure Dad'll come in for the whole day soon."

"You think so?"

"If I've learned anything about him in my lifetime, yes. I'd hoped he'd get back into working a little at a time, but certainly didn't hold my breath." She reached over the counter and tapped the sign taped to the front.

"He really believes every word of this. It's become his motto."

Hank leaned over to peruse the words Dad had clipped when the local newspaper published one of President Roosevelt's Fireside Chats.

Here are three high purposes for every American:

```
1. We shall not stop work for a sin-
   gle day. If any dispute arises we
   shall keep on working while the
   dispute is solved by mediation,
   conciliation, or arbitration - un-
   til the war is won.
2. We shall not demand special gains
   or special privileges or special
```

> advantages for any one group or occupation.
> 3. We shall give up conveniences and modify the routine of our lives if our country asks us to do so. We will do it cheerfully, remembering that the common enemy seeks to destroy every home and every freedom in every part of our land.

This generation of Americans has come to realize, with a present and personal realization, that there is something larger and more important than the life of any individual or of any individual group - something for which a man will sacrifice, and gladly sacrifice, not only his pleasures, not only his goods, not only his associations with those he loves, but his life itself. In time of crisis when the future is in the balance, we come to understand, with full recognition and devotion, what this Nation is, and what we owe to it.

Franklin Delano Roosevelt
February, 1942

"That's Roy's motto for sure. Well, I'll do my best with him."

"I know you will, but really, our hands are tied. He'd rather die working than sitting around." She closed the dilapidated record book as the back door announced Dad's entrance. Before Hank went back to work, she added, "I'm so glad we're in this together."

The peculiar lift of his right eyebrow stayed with her all afternoon, along with his parting words. "Why don't you go home early today? Your dad and I can handle any customers that come in." His seriousness came through without sounding bossy.

"Maybe I will. I've got the books caught up, and the garden still needs lots of attention."

At three o'clock, Hank came over to the counter and waited for her to look up. When she did, he slanted his head. "So, are you going home or not?"

The humor in his tone made her grin. "Guess I could. It's a pretty slow day—maybe I'll stop by the rendering works for some lard."

Out front, a rising wind rattled the garage sign and sent an inner tube flying from the rubber pile. She scurried after the dirty, flopping tube, hoping the truck driver who picked up rubber from collection depots in the surrounding towns showed up pretty soon. The heap grew by the day, including toy balls, used rubber bed sheets, and raincoats. Some patriotic little girl even left her baby doll.

Dad had scoured the shed and basement as soon as the first call for rubber went out. "Good we got something to offer—never dreamed they could use this stuff in airplanes and life rafts. I've offered the garage as a collection depot, just so you know."

Glenora dusted off her hands and turned to survey the sign again. With another strong storm, it might fall apart completely. She'd forgotten all about fixing it, and Slim must've, too. He'd kept his distance from the shop while Dad had been sick.

The scum on the front window allowed only a dim view of the inside, but she knew what Hank and Dad were working on. During his illness, she and Hank had arrived at a balance without even discussing the workload. Having Dad here all day tomorrow would almost seem abnormal.

Turning the corner, she ran into Tillie Murphy, her old high school friend.

"Hey, Glenora. Haven't seen you for ages."

"Same here, but it's no wonder—all I do is work these days."

"Me, too, especially since John's been called up now. I hoped against hope, but I guess having almost two children to support doesn't count to Uncle Sam anymore." She patted her burgeoning midsection. "I know people think John should've enlisted when everyone else around here did, but..."

The morning men's circle discussed that sentiment one day, but Glenora had paid no attention. "Will you move back in with your folks now?"

"Haven't decided yet, but most likely. I can't live on nothing. Oughta become more independent, but..." Again, Tillie smoothed her hand over her middle.

"Well, I'd better get on home."

"Someone said your dad's been sick?"

"Uh-huh. But he's better now. You take care, Tillie."

"Say, how about doing something together some day— maybe go down to Mason City?"

The wind blew Tillie's felt hat off, and Glenora caught it against the side of the building. "Whoosh—I guess winter's not so far away. If I ever get a day off, that sounds good, but things are awfully busy..."

"Let me know, all right? We wouldn't have to go anywhere, really...maybe we could just fix each other's hair."

"Hmm...well, you could fix mine, at least. Don't know if I could make yours into a better victory roll than you already have."

"I've thought of becoming a beauty operator, you know, and your thick hair would be glorious to work with. That wave would be gorgeous if you'd let it fall over your eye, you know."

"Well, we'll see." Glenora waved and hurried down the street. What on earth was Tillie talking about? Who had time to spend over their hair? The next thing, she'd propose going to a movie, as Slim Anderson did again the week before Dad got sick. "Hank needs to get out, Glenora, after all he's been through. How about you and him take in a movie some night?"

She hadn't given him the satisfaction of a response. Why would she want to see a movie, when most of them featured war stories? Who needed to see a sailor falling for a native girl on some island? The nightly news reports supplied more than enough information about the war, not to mention the men hanging around the shop. Sometimes, the imaginations the constant input created taunted her through the night. She ran Red's last letter through her mind.

Never thought I'd see an actual jungle. Hotter n' blazes here.

I'd be rich if somebody'd buy mosquitoes by the pound. Wish I'd paid more attention in geography class—if you see Mr. Hendrickson, tell him I said so, okay?

Don't worry about me. We all take care of each other here, and your letters cheer me up, Glen.

Glenora gulped. Letters—she'd been remiss this past week. Better write to Red tonight.

"Heard y' been around the block a time 'r two, Hank."

Silence, except for the insistent twisting of metal on metal. Finally, Hank emerged from a farm truck's underbelly, a wrench in one hand and a small piece of metal in the other. He heaved himself up from the floor and held out whatever it was, completely ignoring the wizened farmer's broad hint for information.

"Here's your problem, Elmer. Got any idea how this ended up in your fuel line?"

"Well, I'll be schniggered. Who knows? Got a couple young fellas helpin' out from the camp over at Algona—Germans, y' know. Pris'ners—same ones that been helpin' your uncle. Cheap labor, and they seem happy to work. Pay 'em in scrip, y'know, and they got a place in the camp to buy everyday stuff."

He caught his thumb in his bib overalls. "Say, y' don't think them Germans woulda done this to a fella's machine t' vex a fella, do y'?"

Hank's color darkened three shades during Elmer's little speech, but he made no reply. He closed his eyes on the word *Germans*, and when Elmer paused, took a deep breath. Glenora couldn't help but watch...and she pinpointed the exact moment he found control.

Now she knew Hank had fought in North Africa—what must it be like for him to think of German POWs living so close? Seeing his expression change, she recognized the same flagrant emotion that filled his eyes the night Dad had his spell.

At the time, all she could think of was getting Doc here

as fast as possible. But now, Hank's expression was clear—a mix of fear and concern.

All alone here while she ran for Doc, had Hank thought Dad was dying? And now this—how could this customer be so heartless? Hank probably already knew about the prisoners an hour west of here, but why bring up the subject? The local talk was that the captured Germans' labor saved the day for some farmers, and they seemed to cause no trouble.

These thoughts took Glenora back overseas. *What if Red's a prisoner? What if the Japs have him by now?* She had no idea who would treat him worse, the Nazis or the Japanese. And then she realized Hank might have been captured, too—it wasn't unheard of for soldiers to escape and make it back to the States.

He came over and bent his head toward her, his warmth blending with the oily scent on his hands. His voice seemed more hushed than usual, even though Elmer loudly engaged Dad in talk about the weather.

"No need to call your dad away from patching that tire, Glenora. We ought to charge this guy seventy-five cents for the parts and a dollar for the labor, I'd say." He sought her eyes. "Does that sound about right to you?"

A tingle traced her spine, but she shook it off and gathered her senses. "Sure does. Thanks."

He lingered another few seconds, just enough to ignite a wave of concern. Without thinking, she touched his sleeve. "Are you doing okay, Hank?"

The flicker in his eyes answered for him, so she expressed her uneasiness. "I sure wish people would stop talking about the war and those POWS in Algona. I hear enough from the radio as it is, don't you?"

He studied her for a few moments as if no one else were in the garage. Hank seemed to forget the work that called him, too, and his intensity forced Glenora to reckon with the deep splash of indigo in his eyes.

Her stomach did a flip-flop when he finally whispered, "Yeah, plenty enough."

Then he visibly shook himself before setting to work on the motorcycle Howard Turney brought in this morning in a panic. Howard had tripped over some rubber items left beside the raised garage door and stumbled in breathless. He practically ran into Hank, who'd just completed another job and was about to begin another.

"Oh, you're that new mechanic, right?" Howard gave Hank no time to reply. "Think you can help me out? Heard you figure things out fast, and I gotta get this thing runnin' by day after tomorrow for my trip to Fort Dodge. Can't put it off, since it's for the war board down there. This bike takes a lot less gas than a car."

Making no promises, Hank bent to examine the cycle. Howard fidgeted the whole time, until with no promise of success, Hank said he'd give it a try.

Elmer finally let Dad go back to work on some wiring—light work, the kind that involved no lifting or ducking under a vehicle. Hank had brought the project to him earlier, before he disappeared under the farm truck.

"Sorta like a switchboard, Mr. Carson, but this particular configuration got run together somehow—baffles me. Could you figure it out while I work underneath?"

His expertise touched Glenora—he made it seem like Dad was helping him. Now, Elmer sauntered over to the counter. Maybe he'd be the first customer today to pay on the spot.

No matter how few doled out their money on the same day they drove their vehicle away, she always held out hope.

35

Chapter Four

Dear Brother of mine,

A little bird told me you've been under the weather, so I'm inviting myself over for dinner on Thanksgiving. We'll be there about noon, and tell Glenora we'll bring the turkey and trimmings.

Gerold's family will come from Charles City, too, so there'll be eight of us altogether, although I'll bring plenty for Tom and his family, if he can get away.

See you soon, and take care of yourself,
Henrietta

Glenora read the note Dad threw down on the kitchen table. "You told her?"

"Dad, she's your sister. And your episode scared me to death."

"Whaddya mean, *episode?*"

"That's what Doc called it, and with his experience, I assume he knows what he's talking about. Don't you?"

"Them high-falutin' doctors and lawyers think they run this country. But right now, they're findin' out who's really in charge—men of fighting age."

"I wouldn't call Doc high-falutin', would you? It's not like he's a surgeon down in Des Moines or somewhere. And he's never acted better than anybody else around here, that I know of—besides that, he did his part in the Great War, didn't he?"

"Yeah. I just…"

Glenora could visualize his mental gears shifting. Putting into words his own fear never came easy. As often happened at such times, Mama's voice entered her thoughts. *Your father's like all other men, dear. He hides his emotions, and things have to seem like his idea. Even if he knows I thought of something first, he claims it, especially if it ends up working.*

Probably most of Halberton's marriages functioned with that premise in mind, but that didn't make it right. Why did the man always have to occupy first place?

Another one of those things she might as well accept, though they chafed at her sense of justice, especially when she'd proven she could do men's work. Dad flung one last statement her way before he left for the shop.

"By the way, I think I'll invite Hank for Thanksgiving dinner, too.."

"Fine, but I assumed Slim and Minnie would ask him out to the farm."

"Well, at least he'll have a choice this way."

As Dad crossed the porch, Glenora pulled back the yellow gingham curtains to look over the back yard. Nothing much left to see, since she'd burned the last of the dried-up garden last evening. Sparks meeting the darkening sky and the pungent smell of burning leaves had been a treat, even though her side ached from helping Dad hold up the front quarter of a car while Hank performed some miracle with the axle.

When he emerged from under the behemoth, Hank noticed her and grimaced. "Sorry, maybe we should've…"

Dad interrupted. "Nah, this saved an hour for us. Don't worry about Glenora—she's tough."

Hank bit his lip, and his eyes darkened. He glanced at her, opened his mouth to say something, but decided against it. Glenora tucked away this moment, a small treasure in the midst of such a gloomy month, with the sun pretending this part of the earth didn't exist.

November had always seemed longer than any other month except March, which went on forever. But having company coming for Thanksgiving gave her something to look forward to—menus to plan, rooms to clean. Dad hadn't really meant his angry outburst about Henrietta, she knew that.

What piqued him was that she'd done it without him being aware, and in the process, revealed something he'd rather keep under wraps. It was that age-old truth Mama had shared, that a man needs to come up with ideas for them to be acceptable. Well, truth be told, dad would never have thought of issuing the invitation, although under his bristly exterior, he looked forward to having relatives here next Thursday, too.

Two years of working around men had reinforced Mama's insight. Hearing the men of Halberton air their ideas at the garage taught her to listen with discernment—sometimes they were just spouting off. And she'd learned to pay attention to those who had little to say...or nothing at all, like Hank.

She took up Aunt Henrietta's letter again. Of course she was coming—hadn't Mama always called Henrietta Dad's favorite sister? Her carefully penned lines brought a certain satisfaction, though Glenora couldn't exactly put her finger on it. She folded the letter in thirds to return its envelope. That was when she spied the note on the back.

Glenora—I'm looking forward to some time with you. If you don't mind, I'd like to stay overnight. What do you say we head over to Mason City on Friday morning? I haven't gone shopping for a long time, and am betting you could use a few things, too.

Leave it to Aunt Henrietta to think she might need something. When Mama took sick, it was Henrietta who drove all the way down here with homemade bread and chicken noodle soup. She spent three days helping out, and before she left, presented Glenora with a new pleated wool skirt and cardigan.

"Thought you might not have taken time to prepare for the opening of school...hope this fits." It did, and having that one new outfit to wear perked Glenora up during those dismal weeks of Mama's illness.

The kitchen hadn't changed much since then, even the way she'd just stacked the dishes in the tall cupboard Mama had inherited from her grandmother. A place for everything, and everything in its place. The sameness might be boring to others, but the old pump over the dishpan and worn yellow linoleum covering fir floorboards eased Glenora's spirit. She wasn't sure she'd want anything to change, since every inch of this room brought Mama to mind.

This linoleum, the newest thing ten years ago, covered all but a foot square around the periphery of the room, but the brown and turquoise flourishes had faded into pale replicas. Could it be almost four years since that awful day Doc witnessed Mama's last breath and announced that she had passed from this world?

With the war and all, there didn't seem to be much reason to update anything. Red would want everything exactly like it was when he left...that's what Mama would say.

They hadn't heard from him in six weeks—strange, since the war officially ended on September 2. The last he wrote, his ship suffered irrevocable damage in a typhoon that swept through Buckner Bay, otherwise known as Nakagusuku Wan. Some sailors were lost, too, and Dad voiced surprise that the censors had let that line pass without blacking it out. Another ship took Red and the others on, but he hadn't given its name. Maybe he couldn't.

That irritated Dad, who had spent every evening listening for the name of Red's original ship. One more link to him gone—that was the way of war. Glenora's sigh swept the kitchen as she went to get dressed. Even though Ernie Pyle did his best to keep you updated, you never really knew what was going on.

Aunt Henrietta's note jogged Glenora's memory. Shopping together always gave her hope back in high school, when what she wore mattered. Aunt Henrietta's mannerisms, her nervous little chuckle and her tendency to jump into arguments at her own expense made her seem Mama's sister instead of her sister-in-law.

But with things as they were around here, could she afford a morning off? Glenora's thoughts flitted to Hank, who probably greeted Dad right now over at the garage. She could imagine him presenting some mechanical conundrum and pretending he needed help—his practiced tactic to keep Dad from under the vehicles as much as possible.

Knowing he had things under control at the shop, she spent an hour shaping up the house—Thanksgiving would be here in less than a week. An hour later, with a load of clothes soaking in the Maytag washer, including the sheets for the extra bedroom, she dusted the headboard and chest.

If the weather stayed mild, she'd better remember to air out this room next Wednesday.

She cleared the spare rod in the closet, noting a shiny rose swatch that stood out from the rest of the clothing. One touch took her back to her junior prom. With Mama so ill, Aunt Henrietta took her shopping for it in Mason City. In the J C Penney dressing room mirror, she *oohed* and *aahed* over this dress, saying how its lines emphasized Glenora's slim shoulders.

"Come out here and take a look in the three-way mirror. You've got to have a pair of long gloves, of course. How about these?" She pronounced the third pair Glenora tried on perfect. "Yes, these squiggles—must be some elastic sewn in there—they draw the eye up, away from..."

"My big ankles. I know."

Aunt Henrietta took Glenora back into the dressing room and held her face between her hands. "If you haven't noticed, you have feet and ankles exactly like mine—strong. You and I are longer-faced, tall women. But that certainly didn't stop your uncle Bill from pursuing me, and it won't stop some lucky young man from choosing you, Glenora Carson."

The satiny fabric felt cool against Glenora's cheek, and the style fit her—not fancy, but elegant. On prom night, she discovered Aunt Henrietta was right—Joe liked her dress. He even vowed that he wanted to spend the rest of his life with her. Months later, out behind the house on the night before he boarded the train for the West Coast, he asked her to wait for him.

"I considered holding off until I get back, honey. But then— well, my heart won out over my head, so I'm asking you now." He took a ring from his pocket and the moonlight caught its natural sparkle.

"This isn't the kind of ring you deserve, but I..." Joe squeezed her hand. "It's to say I'll think of you every single day, and we'll get married as soon as I get off that ship and cross the country. Will you wait for me, Glen?"

Now, Glenora whispered her reply into the folds of the dress. "Of course, Joe." For such a long time, she'd denied herself the luxury of tears, but allowed them to flow today. "There'll never be anyone quite like you. I hope you know that. But it's been years now, and..."

An empty sensation rode her breastbone—maybe these memories had lost some of their power. When a knock sounded downstairs, she stepped back, letting the dreamy dress float into the closet's dark recesses. Like her memories... and her commitment to Joe Lundene.

"This one. I liked the yellow one on you, but it did tint your skin a little orange, dear."

Glenora stared into the long dressing room mirror of the Damon's Department Store lady's department. A deep rose shirtwaist blouse shimmered back at her under the double-stitched dark grey and white tweed suit she'd tried on at Aunt Henrietta's urging. She pivoted and walked a few feet, noting how the skirt made room for her long stride.

"Do you think the flare suits my legs? I got used to permanent pleats, and now..."

"Why, yes. Women of all ages wear the new A-line flare these days. It's such a flattering style."

"But with the war and everything...?"

"That's why pleats went out and A-lines came into vogue. You should buy this suit, dear. Couldn't be more perfect—fits

you to a T. And the color goes with your dark hair and por-
celain skin."

What Aunt Henrietta saw in Glenora's expression caused
her to add more details. "For heaven's sake, child, if anybody
deserves something new, it's you. How long has it been since
you even walked into a store?"

Glenora couldn't remember. But she had to admit that
trying on this suit produced a glow she hadn't experienced
for a long time. The small front pocket and little tucks on
the bodice added just the right feminine touch. Today had
nothing to do with broken starters, unruly sparkplugs, or
complaining customers. The air in the store exuded fabric
dye, perfume, new shoe and purse leather.

An hour earlier, walking toward Federal Avenue past
the Park Inn Hotel across from the park, she'd felt swept
clean—like their house for the holidays. Beside her, Aunt
Henrietta, who had always seemed young for her age, picked
up speed.

"I can't wait to get into the store, Glenora. Shopping with
you has always been so much fun. I love my boys, but you've
always seemed like the daughter I wished for."

Swept clean—free from confusing paperwork, curmudgeonly farmers, bills to pay, and the ever-present concern
about rubber and gasoline rationing. Plus the underlying
anxiety that some clients might never pay Dad what they
owed him—not to mention Dad's health.

And then there was her constant concern about Red.
Though still aware that enormous trouble lay only one tele-
graph away, Glenora breathed deeper today. The sights and
sounds of the city's busy main street energized her. Next to
Damon's sat the First National Bank, still sporting bullet

holes from the famous Dillinger robbery in '34, and import-ant-looking folks dressed in business finery milled on the sidewalks.

No, she would refuse any of her energy to worry today. Aunt Henrietta seemed bent on the same goal. "So, you'll take this blouse, too? That deep rose brings out your eyes, you know, like your prom dress. And with a bright hat, you'll look fabulous—how about this one?"

She reached to a mannequin for a matching felt specimen. "See how that heightens the hue in your cheeks?"

At her bidding, Glenora twirled around, and she had to say, this suit made her feel like a woman. She'd been a girl when her aunt took her shopping for her prom dress, but the years had increased her curves. In the end, she secured both the dress and the hat. Aunt Henrietta added a pair of low black heels, even though Glenora argued that hers were still serviceable.

"Besides, I never go anywhere fancy enough to wear..."

"Oh, pshaw! Consider these a Christmas gift from me. Let me treat you. You look spectacular in this outfit. After all, you do need something to wear to church, don't you?"

"I'd been thinking of re-working something of Mama's, actually."

"And exactly when would you find time to do that? From what I can see, you're already working two full-time jobs. And doing them both well, I might add. Do you get any pay for your work at the garage, Nora?"

"No, but..."

"Well, your dad *owes* you this, at the very least. I've known him way longer than you, and he's a wizard at making do. Surviving the Depression taught us all that. But I also know

Roy would bend over backwards to make his little girl happy, and your mother wouldn't want you looking shabby."

"You think I look shabby?"

"We all do, when we stop paying attention to ourselves. There's a time for everything, Nora, and today's the time to look forward."

When they headed east out of Mason City, the gloomy weather hadn't changed a bit, sweeping a cold wind across barren corn and soybean rows. Meager-looking pheasants gleaned nubbins from the near-barren plant stubs. The only variation in color came where farmers had already plowed the earth. New rows of tall wooden light poles staggered down rutted country roads on both sides of the main route to Osage, their unspoken message loud and clear. In spite of the war, change still strode this land like a determined giant. It wouldn't be long and every home in town would boast a telephone, Slim said, and the farmhouses, too.

Turning toward home, Aunt Henrietta tossed her head and let loose with the lyrics of a popular tune. *I'll be seeing you...* She glanced over at Glenora. "I love that new song, and Harry James' orchestra in general."

The words always made Glenora sad, but she declined to say so. Her aunt continued, "Apple blossom time—that's when Bill and I got married, and your Mama and Daddy, too. This old war will end one day, and we'll all take up living again."

She turned onto the Red Ball road. "I suppose some folks would say I've wasted gasoline, driving down here to see you. But I've been saving up my coupons for weeks, and I miss you and your dad. I looked into the mirror last week and told myself, 'You need an outing, old girl.' We all deserve a little something special once in a while."

"Well, you've certainly given me something special today—thank you. I needed to see you, too—I didn't realize how much until today. I'm so glad you made the effort."

Aunt Henrietta twisted her head. "Your letter spurred me to come, of course. But even in wartime, there's such a thing as being too careful, don't you think? We only get to live once, and with your Dad having that spell…"

She straightened her shoulders against the leather seat and fed the car more gas. "Of course, he won't even listen when I mention it, but that's just his stubborn manhood." She veered around a curve and straightened out the wheel. "Well, I'll just say that I've never regretted following my instincts when it comes to staying in touch with family."

It wasn't until late Friday afternoon when she and Dad saw Henrietta off from the front porch that Glenora allowed a realization to sink in. Hank hadn't come for dinner yesterday. Although she basked in the time with her aunt, a twinge of disappointment tiptoed just below her breastbone.

Chapter Five

"Christmas 1944. We come here at this holy time with high hopes for peace. And for our boys still over there in the jungles, on the sea, in Europe's dense forests, or in the Far East, we lift our prayers for peace."

The sermon went on and on. After ten minutes, a snore erupted next to Glenora, so she gave Dad an automatic jab in the ribs. He shook himself awake and muttered, "Wish we had our regular preacher back. This fella don't know when to stop."

Glenora agreed, but the war affected churches, too. Reverend Avery signed up for the chaplaincy on the most recent draft of older men. She gave Dad's comment a quiet, *Um hum*. Thankfully, only a few candles glowed throughout the sanctuary tonight, so most folks didn't even notice.

After the main service, the pastor announced, "We decided to skimp on the candlelight service tonight, keeping in mind that every sacrifice we make multiplies thousands of times over for our young men far from home. But let no one doubt the love burning in our hearts that keeps them going."

"Not to mention our prayers—we cannot pray enough for those boys, and may I add, the many nurses now in harm's way. When we rise in the night, distraught with anxiety, the one thing we can do for them is lift our voices to heaven."

Dad's head slipped against Glenora's shoulder, but before she could react, someone jolted him from his other side. She leaned forward in time to notice Hank's grin. So he'd come after all—she'd overheard Slim urge Dad to invite him one day at the shop.

"You know what he's gone through, Roy. I've kept that quiet except from you. It'd do a lot of good for him to attend a service on Christmas Eve. After what his..."

Just then, Hank had revved an automobile engine on the other side of the shop, so Slim's last word faded. Something like *wife*, but that couldn't be it.

When Glenora questioned Dad about the conversation that evening after he turned off the radio, he merely pursed his lips. Then he shot her a question.

"Slim said he was driving Minnie down to Ottumwa to their son's for Christmas. Think maybe we should invite Hank along for Christmas dinner?"

He had turned completely her way, suddenly attentive to the movement of her needle through one of his work socks. "Do you want to?'

"If he's going to be alone, sure. Nobody should spend Christmas alone."

He went to bed, so she left the decision to him. As he padded to the back bedroom in his stockinged feet, a thought occurred to her: what would he do in the evenings when the war ended, with no more war reports to focus on? Hopefully, he'd play checkers with Red until he gained some grandchildren.

The next night, Dad said, "Hank's driving over to his folks' place on Christmas Day."

Hmm... must just be going for the day. Glenora couldn't remember where they lived, or maybe Hank hadn't mentioned that detail.

She shook off thoughts of him and lifted her eyes to the candle glowing above the altar. "If You could please bring Red home to us... that's all I ask."

Back at home, Dad laid out everything they'd need for the drive to Aunt Henrietta's son's house in Charles City for Christmas dinner. Even Tom and his family were coming for the meal. Suddenly, Dad seemed full of energy.

"Been a long time since I drove the bubbletop. It'll do the old transmission good to get the rust out of her system."

Seeing him excited about something did Glenora's heart good, but as she went to bed, a familiar taunt cast its shadow. Christmas, and still no word from Red.

On the twenty-fifth, Aunt Henrietta met them at her son Gerold's house in Charles City. "I'm so happy to see you all, and thrilled you could get away, Roy." The package she handed him contained a flannel bathrobe. As soon as Glenora opened one end of her gift, she knew what it was.

"You didn't!"

"Couldn't help myself, honey. The day after Thanksgiving, I knew you needed shoes more than this, but you looked simply splendid in this royal blue."

Bright white polka dots on a shiny poplin shirtwaist background—Glenora could hardly believe her eyes. The lush cloth brushed against her hand—smoother than velvet, smoother than a freshly painted chassis.

That day in Damon's, Aunt Henrietta had pronounced

this flowing skirt ideal for her long legs. Now, she drew the whole room's attention to Glenora.

"Go on! Try it on for us."

"Come on, Aunt G'Nora. I'll try on my new outfit, too." It was hard to turn down Anna, her sweet ten-year-old niece. The two of them changed in the bedroom and put on a style show.

Dad's eyes lit up, though he kept his sentiments quiet. Tom's wife Nancy snapped a picture of them with her new Brownie camera. "I'll send you a copy when we get them developed, all right?"

The drive home took longer than on the way over, since Dad detoured around a couple of used car lots. "Gotta keep an eye out, you know. Never know when there might be somethin' I'll need, and they might have just the thing." He got out at both lots, so Glenora walked around with him.

"Over there—the one with its hood up—ain't that a Nash just like Homer Brenaw's? Been lookin' for a clutch for that car for..."

"About a year now."

"Yeah." He shinnied over a four-foot fence like a youth and wound through a maze of rusty abandoned vehicles. Glenora, skirt or no skirt, clambered after him, but by the time she arrived at the Nash, her dad was head first down under the seat. She held her breath—if something happened to his heart out here, what would she do?

But a few minutes later, he scrambled out with a metal piece in his hand. His face's brilliant flush gradually receded, but it took the entire way to the truck for his breathing to return to normal.

Five minutes down the road, he spouted a question.

"Wouldn't wonder if Hank's still on his way home from Sioux Center—that's a long drive. Supposed to be back to work tomorrow, ain't he?"

"He said he would be."

Dad's shrug brought no satisfaction, and the click of his bedroom door left Glenora alone in the living room. After the bustling day, the house seemed all too quiet. She pulled her new dress out of its box and held it up to her shoulders. The hall mirror could not lie. The deep blue emphasized her eyes—Aunt Henrietta was right.

Standing there in the hallway, a sudden awareness swept over her. She couldn't wait to see Hank in the morning.

"Over here, Glenora. Bring another yard of that tissue. Can't have our main fundraising banner look bare and dull."

When Glenora complied, Effie Peterson gave a nod. "So glad to see you here, dear. These fundraisers are the least we can do for our troops, and having one on New Year's Eve was a brilliant idea." She sniffed. "Although I hate to give Eloise McCall credit for it."

Her comment brought back the quiet feud the whole town knew she and Eloise waged. Mama used to shake her head and say, "Effie and Eloise are like Mutt and Jeff, opposites trying to run the church kitchen."

But such good memories sprang from having Effie next door. She always had a friendly word or a big sugar cookie to offer, often accompanied by her strong opinion about something or other. And if she saw your shoulders slumping, she invited you in for coffee and a chat.

Effie must miss Mama—they'd shared so many woes in

each other's kitchen. More often than not, they talked over the garden fence or shared a break on the front porch when the children came home from school. Back in those days, Glenora played paper dolls or hide-and-seek with Audrey Peterson and her sister Penny until suppertime.

A quick sweep of the school gymnasium revealed more people entering. Effie dragged a chair over to Glenora. "Thanks to your height, I think we can finish this off without a stepladder, dear. It's a blessing to be tall, I've always said."

In a couple of minutes, Glenora secured the banner in place, just in time for a surge of townspeople and farm families. Plenty of folks she hadn't seen for a long time, and the hot cider cauldron proved a good place to greet them. One by one, they stopped by to talk, including some of her elementary or high school teachers. Seeing them with their husbands or wives reminded her of her adult state.

Except I'm not married with children. This old war made sure of that.

On the stage, Roma Ross and her husband still arranged chairs and instruments for a local band. George Miller brought in his accordion, and two men shoved an upright piano into position. The sparkle of a trumpet and saxophone flashed in the burning lightbulbs hanging from the ceiling, and an amateur started warming up the group.

Then someone unlocked a side door and even more people streamed in. At fifty cents a ticket, success appeared inevitable. Slim and Minnie showed up and Slim hurried over to Glenora. "Your dad here tonight?"

"You know better than that. He couldn't miss a news broadcast. But maybe it's a good thing—this way, he'll be resting."

"What about Hank?"

"I wouldn't know. Look around, maybe he came, maybe not."

"Well, he went to church with you, so I figured…"

"Slim. Stop figuring, all right?"

At her tone, Slim took a step back. Glenora put her hands on her hips. "Hank's a grown man and doesn't need you planning his social life. And neither do I." Her sharpness surprised her—when had she spoken to anyone this way?

Slim's eyebrows sank into his forehead. "I'm only trying to help him out. He's had a rough row to hoe."

"But he's doing well. He's found a good job, and has a way with impatient customers, too, and with Dad. I don't know what I'd have done without him when Dad had that spell."

Slim brightened, so she softened her earlier outburst. "You've been so good to Dad over the years, and I know he appreciates your friendship."

Slim smoothed his hand over his chest and exhaled.

"But the truth is, Slim, some people dig their heels in the more you push them. Dad's like that, you know."

"That's for sure. I s'pose you're right. I oughta mind my own business. But I just can't help…"

"For our first song, folks, we've chosen a recent Mills Brothers' release, 'You Always Hurt the One You Love.' This tune came out in October, and has topped the charts ever since. After that, you'll hear our rendition of 'Don't Fence Me In' by the Andrews sisters and Bing Crosby. Stay tuned for many more as the evening progresses."

The school superintendent, standing next to the band leader, straightened his tie and bellowed into a heavy cardboard megaphone. "Let me point out these five lovely girls up front, everyone. They've consented to rent themselves out for dances. A quarter a dance, and all the money goes for the war effort. So you shy fellows, here's your chance to shine.

"Do it for the cause. Get out there and dance, and when you're hungry, the First Methodist ladies, the Lutheran Ladies Circle, and the Knights of Columbus have just what you need in the line of food and drink over on the south wall."

Slim pulled his hands from his pockets. "Well, then. I'd better get over there and take Minnie out to dance."

Someone touched Glenora's elbow. "Wheredja get that gorgeous dress? You look as stylish as Barbara Stanwyck, and here I am, as big as a pickle barrel. Come on out and dance with me. I already bought us two tickets." Tillie's glowing hazel eyes belied the discomfort she must feel.

"You're going to dance?"

"Absolutely. I didn't draw seams down the backs of my legs for nothing. There's not a pair of silk stockings to be found these days, and I ought to know. Drove all the way to Mason City, but in vain. John told me not to sit around at home. With his folks watching little Toby tonight, I see this as a way to contribute to the war effort. Speaking of that, have you gotten a Victory Cookbook yet?"

At Glenora's headshake, Tillie pulled her onto the dance floor and moved her feet to the music. "You get one when you buy LYSOL, and it's chock full of one-dish dinners. Saves time for women who have to work now, with a frankfurter casserole, even soybean and peanut recipes. Have you heard how they're even rationing horse meat in some places?"

Glenora made a face. Aware that she towered over Tillie by a good six inches, she felt ridiculous out here, but attempted to follow Tillie's movements.

"Cross my heart. Anyway, back to the cookbook. John's

mother already tried the meat and vegetable pie—yummy. *Uncle Sam needs us strong,* don't you know?"

Tillie lost her balance momentarily and laughed at her awkwardness. "Maybe this'll help the baby come sooner. The day Toby was born, I washed the car, and that seemed to work. Oh, look—there's Cynthia Jannes. Can't believe she came, with what they..."

Whatever she saw cross Glenora's face stopped her. "Oh. Well, I don't want to dwell on bad news. Let's go get some punch."

A while later, Tillie found another victim, so Glenora sought Cynthia out. "Good to see you. How are things going?"

Tears glinted in Cynthia's eyes. "My brother Ed's in that horrible fight in Italy. The battles are fierce, and last forever. I know we have to take Rome, but we heard Ed's been wounded. Waiting for word is driving my folks crazy. Sometimes, the tension makes me want to scream. Did you ever think, back when we were young, we'd have to go through something like this?"

"No, I never did."

"What do you hear from Red?"

It took less than half a minute to answer, and Glenora knew her glistening eyes matched Cynthia's. No amount of dancing could change that, though she tried to focus on the red, white and blue poster hanging on the far wall.

Our Lives Our Fortunes Our Resources
Preparedness
Liberty
Thanks God – We're Americans

A golden statue of liberty connected the words *preparedness* and *liberty*. Four emblems—an airplane, a ship, a tank, and a cannon crossed the banner's bottom.

Cynthia drew herself up. "Well, at least we have our work. Someday my life will return to normal, although it sure doesn't seem like that'll happen anytime soon."

At least we have our work... Someone asked Cynthia to dance, and Glenora leaned against the wall, tapping her foot absentmindedly. Her graduation scholarship passed through her mind. Cynthia had always wanted to be a secretary, and enjoyed her position with a local lawyer, but the future suddenly yawned before Glenora like an endless chasm.

Would she spend the rest of her life at the garage, when she'd once envisioned teaching home economics? She had no idea, since Red's return would make all the difference. What if he came home minus a leg, an arm, or worse? Then what would he do—she couldn't imagine him being satisfied taking over the bookwork.

She rearranged the cider cups as the band swung into yet another song. Her dream of teaching had gone out the window with her scholarship—even if Red came home whole, how could she ever afford college?

An hour and a half before midnight, some of the older couples drifted home. With the door opening and closing, the high-ceilinged room filled with drafts. Glenora sought her cardigan and when one of the food ladies stifled a yawn, offered to take over for her at the pies. The woman gave a relieved sigh.

"You're a blessing, Glenora, you know that? My feet are killing me."

A little later, Tillie stopped by to say goodnight and left. Glenora rehearsed their conversation. *Women who have to work now...* she couldn't remember not working. Once again, her scholarship flashed before her—no use thinking about that.

Every fifteen minutes, the announcer counted down to midnight. "Forty-five minutes left, folks. Time to dig deep for the cause."

When he announced half an hour, Glenora counted the money the church had raked in—nearly a hundred dollars. Earlier, they almost ran short on food, and a couple of women ran home to see what they could find—one returned with cookies and a cake, and another offered part of a mincemeat pie. They also got the grocery store owner to open up so they could buy more coffee.

Minus zero temperatures helped with those sales, and the apple cider ran out, too. On a wooden folding chair, Glenora watched the crowd—mostly girls dancing together, since a good share of the men were fighting. But at ten minutes before twelve, someone whispered in her ear.

"About time you danced, don't you think? That dress was made for it."

Her heart leapt. She'd know that voice anywhere. Hank added, "If you dance with me, it'll keep Slim off our backs for a while."

"But I promised to watch the food... and Slim took Minnie home an hour ago."

Hank pulled her up and guided her onto the floor with a firm hand to her lower back. "Yeah, but he'll hear, trust me. He hears everything. Especially about me."

"Is there a lot to hear?" Glenora put her left hand on Hank's shoulder and fell into his smooth rhythm, surprised at his grace.

"That depends how you look at it, I guess." He angled his head and puckered his brow, so she expected a serious answer. But he chuckled. "I'm pretty famous, but do my best to keep the news at a minimum." He twirled her around, and when their hands met again, she felt glamorous, even pretty.

The final countdown to midnight drowned out whatever Hank said to her, but it couldn't hide the glint in his eyes. A few minutes later, he helped her clean up and walked her home, every bit the gentleman. They talked easily, but as they approached the house, Glenora tried to calm her spinning thoughts.

"Thanks for walking me home. I'm glad you came tonight, and I hope 1945 is good to you."

"It's starting out that way. Thanks for dancing with me, Glenora. Thought maybe you wouldn't know who I was, since I'm not covered with grease."

She chuckled. "Same here."

"Well, at least you're used to my face—that's one thing."

She almost replied *And you're used to mine.*

"If I weren't so tall, that sniper would've hit air instead of mangling me."

"Hank, you're not mangled. And if I weren't so tall, I'd have been asked to dance a lot more in high school."

"Well, whoever didn't ask you was a fool." With that, Hank disappeared, like he had the night he walked her home after Dad's spell.

Between wakefulness and sleep, Glenora heard Dad get up. Long after he returned to his room, she still weighed Hank's every word. *It's starting out that way...* did he mean because they'd been together at midnight?

... used to my face... mangled... whoever didn't ask you was a fool...

As happened often, the old house creaked for no reason at all. Glenora pulled her quilt up around her chin. Yes, she'd definitely gotten used to Hank Anderson's face.

59

Chapter Six

"Our boys've landed on Corregidor, and the Marines have invaded Iwo Jima."

"Owen says them Japs'll be sorry they ever laid eyes on us before this thing's over." Two women chattered in a line at the creamery, where the rich, fatty scent engulfed everything and everyone.

Glenora gave thanks when the women made their purchases and moved outside. Mr. Penning took her order and quickly produced a hand-wrapped package of butter and cream.

"I s'pose you've heard the news—is your brother stationed anywhere near Japan?"

Rather than explaining what she really didn't know, Glenora gave him a simple headshake. All the way home, she spotted people in twos, discussing something or other.

Constant war talk engulfed the garage, too. Over and over, someone repeated the story of the First and Third U.S. Armies meeting up after the Battle of the Bulge. Every rehashing reminded her of Red's silence. Dad must've mentioned it to Hank, because the other day he volunteered to seek information.

"I'm not sure if I could find out anything, but it might be worth a try."

Glenora simply gaped at him. Among millions of enlisted men, with Red separated from his ship, had Hank lost his mind? One insignificant sailor—Red was exactly that, and nothing more. For months now, she'd managed to keep a positive outlook, but Hank's suggestion shook her. Maybe she didn't really want to find out anything.

At the grocer's, she stepped inside. Good to get out of that nasty wind. She headed down the right aisle for a package of Saltines. While she waited to pay, the door opened, bringing in freezing air and causing the old stove to belch out more heat. She considered foregoing the crackers, but she'd planned to take them to work tomorrow with cheese for lunch—something a little different for a change.

A tap on her elbow made her twist, and there stood Cynthia.

"So good to see you again, Glenora. Time sure has flown since that New Year's Eve dance. I don't know if I said so that night, because all I could think about was Ed, but you looked fabulous in that polka-dot dress."

"Um… thanks. Have you heard any more? I think of him every time the newscaster mentions Italy."

"We got a letter last week—boy, I'd begun to wonder. But they sent his platoon to the seaside for a two-day leave, and he took time to write. No details, but he seemed upbeat—just got grazed by a bullet and had recovered."

"Next—step right up." Glenora gave a relieved sigh—no need to answer questions about Red. She really didn't feel up for that today.

After dropping the groceries at home, she studied a mass of February clouds that homed in on Halberton. Because of her birthday, she'd enjoyed February as a child, but now, winter's staleness overshadowed everything. On top of the gloomy weather, the back pasture had become impassable with the last snowstorm.

By the time she reached the front of the garage, a dripping mist began, and she almost failed to recognize someone leaving the Red Cross office down the street. On second look, she realized it was Hank, with something in his hand. Seeing him sent a wave through her, with no time to analyze her instinctive reaction. In an instant, he stood right beside her, with peppermint on his breath.

"Hey, Miss Carson, wait up—got something for you."

She failed to connect what he said with where he'd come from. He studied her face as if he recognized it wasn't her best day, and explained.

"Early in January, I put in a request for word on Red, and something came through today. Seems he's with—well, you can read for yourself."

He handed her a slip of paper and plunged into the shop. Stilling her urge to call him back, Glenora took a deep breath and unfolded the note. She could scarcely take in the news.

Seaman Victor A. Carson, Halberton, IA at latest notice, rescued. Listed heavy cruiser, USS Pensacola, pending reassignment.

Strung together by typewriter keys much in need of cleaning, the words transfixed Glenora. She grabbed the vertical iron handle Dad pounded into the doorframe years ago for times like this when the sidewalks glazed over with ice.

Something in her melted. The backs of her eyes burned, and she couldn't have moved if she'd been fleeing one of those V-1 rockets the Londoners had to contend with. *Red was alive.* All her visions of him buried in shallow sand on some godforsaken island, or worse, at the bottom of the Pacific Ocean, had been mere imaginations.

I've never taught a more imaginative child, Eleanore. Does she take after you?

Mama had come home beaming after her meeting with Glenora's second grade teacher, and from then on, every teacher praised her creativity. But for months now, that imagination had kept her awake at night and forced her into silence by day, lest she worry Dad.

The door opened as she clung to the handle, blinded by her tears. Then she heard an anguished, "Oh, no," and arms twice the size of her fear enveloped her. Grease and tar and rubber never smelled so good as she collapsed against Hank.

"There, there," he whispered, as to a child with a skinned knee. "I thought you'd be—I didn't see anything there but good news."

He held her back a few inches, his eyes moist. "I didn't mean to cause you..."

"No, no. It's just that I've been—I've stayed quiet for Dad, you know?" Her sniffle bade Hank reach for his handkerchief.

"Sorry, this is probably full of sweat."

A half laugh, half moan issued from her mouth. "As long as it's yours, Hank, I don't mind." She blew her nose and a shudder took her, so he gathered her in again.

"Have you told Dad?"

"No, this is your story to tell."

"Red's... Oh, Hank. I was so certain he'd died. I visualized him at... at the bottom of..."

A raw edge entered Hank's voice, and he clasped her wrists. "Enough of that. We can't stop believing, Glenora, no matter what the talk is, no matter how long things take. We've gotta keep trusting your brother'll come home. I've been there, and there's a link somehow. If we stop believing, then..."

She pinched her nose between her thumb and forefinger. "I think you should tell Dad, all right? I trust you more than I trust myself. The last thing he needs is to see me fall apart."

Hank slipped the paper from her hands. "All right, if that's what you want. We'll walk in together, so you'll be right there beside me."

"Yes."

"You're okay now?" The concern in his eyes rattled her, but still warmed her through and through.

"Let me catch my breath a second." She tucked a stray curl into her wool scarf and Hank reached a massive finger to wipe a tear from her cheek. Somehow, she stayed standing, though she grabbed his arm.

Her mind swirled with the news. Halfway over the threshold, she whispered Hank's name, and he turned.

"Thank you. I'm so grateful, I can't even begin to..."

He held that big finger to his lips and pulled her inside, toward the vice-grips, where Roy worked on a stubborn glue job. Besides hearing for sure that Red was alive, another comforting truth attended Glenora. Hank had noticed she didn't come in. And he'd come for her.

"Your dad has a new spring in his step." Aunt Henrietta spoke over the rumble of her Ford and the splash of a steady drizzle. Such a foggy March thirty-first, with Easter day coming so early this year. "He says you still haven't heard any more about Red, but that's all right.

"Sometimes, what he went through in the Great War seems

like a blessing in disguise. Because of that, he understands how impossible it can be to write home."

"I never thought of it that way, but you're usually right."

"Don't you mean *always?*" Henrietta's dimples went into action, and Glenora was struck by how perfectly her widow's peak aligned with her nose and the first button of her crème-colored silk blouse. She'd rarely seen this aunt looking anything less than prim and proper, although when her three boys were young, she must have experienced some hectic days.

"Pretty close, I'd say." Glenora patted the brim of the gift Henrietta presented to her when she arrived yesterday. "Hope you don't mind me horning in on your holiday, folks," she announced as she barged into the living room. "I had everything ready to take to Gerold and his brood, but they came down with late season colds. Called this morning to say they'd better not come—might be the flu."

"So you loaded up everything, and here you are."

"Yes. I figured you probably didn't splurge on an Easter bonnet, Nora, so here's one to go with your polka-dots. What do you think?"

The straw creation boasted a navy blue flower with a splash of bright crimson in the middle and a wide yellow streamer ribbon. Glenora fingered the brim. "Wow—I like it." She put it on and angled her head. "How do I look?"

"Like a woman about town, dear. Perfectly lovely. *I'll be the proudest aaaa-unt in the Easter pa... rade.*"

As usual, Henrietta found a way to get Glenora out of town for a while. "How about driving over with me to see Flo this evening? She sent me an awful lonely letter the other day. It would mean a lot to her to see her niece—and Roy, a visit from you wouldn't hurt, either."

"Count me out." Dad lent his ear to the news again.

"And count me in." A chance to leave town came along only once in a blue moon.

As dusk fell, Henrietta wheeled the seven miles to the farm where her sister Flo had lived alone since her husband died twelve years earlier. Dad probably hadn't seen this sister since the last family funeral. But there was no pulling him away from potential news about Red and the *USS Pensacola*. He'd even gotten out the world atlas and circled Pensacola, Florida.

"D'ja know General Eisenhower demanded the German surrender?" Dad repeated his question for the third time since early that morning when they trooped down the street to the sunrise service.

"I heard, Roy. Wonderful he did this just before Easter—the world definitely needs a resurrection." Aunt Henrietta put a gloved hand on Roy's arm when he missed the first step up to the church.

Luckily, Hank waited there for them. He caught Glenora's eye and sent her a quiet message. At least she thought so. *Don't worry, I've got your dad.*

After the service, he seemed so at ease, even though he'd never met Aunt Henrietta. Her ample ham, scored all around with pineapple rings, provided a real treat, and Glenora knew she'd leave the leftovers here. That would take care of sandwiches for the whole week.

After church, Glenora mashed the potatoes, made gravy and set out the pickles. Sure felt good to eat food she hadn't cooked, for once. Hank helped carry bowls and platters to the table and asked polite questions during the meal.

"So your husband passed years ago, ma'am?"

"Yes, in '33. He made a good living in cement work, but the dust might have contributed to his early death. The two oldest boys and I kept things running for some years, but when the industry started to gear up for the war, we sold out."

She hesitated and gave Roy a glance. "There comes a time to stop working so hard. Maybe we should've kept at it, but honestly, it's a relief not to have to meet quotas and follow government regulations. The boys were able to channel all their experience in other ways, even though that meant they moved away. All-in-all, I'm pleased."

She bit into a scrumptious homemade roll swimming in butter, and Hank attended to his plate, too. Then Henrietta turned the conversation. "So, you've been working with Roy over at the garage?"

Hank nodded as he chewed.

"Did you grow up here? I can't recall your family name."

Glenora jumped in. "Slim and Minnie Anderson—do you remember them?"

"Oh—would their daughter be Elmira?"

"Yes. I'm Slim and Minnie's nephew."

"Ah. Roy, I bet you're mighty glad for the help."

"That's for sure. Did'ja hear…"

Hank set down his fork. "Roy, what do you think we should do about that rattletrap truck Horace Allen brought in yesterday morning? Do you think it's the steering mechanism?"

"Yeah. That sound we heard when we drove around the block told me for sure. Hate t' tear the whole thing apart tomorrow, but we got no choice."

"Right." Hank's eyes locked with Glenora's, and once again, she embraced his silent promise. *I'll take care of your dad.*

"Well, Glenora." Henrietta's eyes glinted at the signs of Roy slipping, but she set her chin. "Time for dessert. It's a new recipe, the highest I've ever seen a cake rise."

After the meal, Hank helped clear the table. "Let me do dishes, will you? I'm pretty good at it."

Henrietta squeezed his elbow. "Oh thank you. But maybe if you stay out with Roy, he'll take a nap. I…" She pressed her hand against her mouth. "I had no idea he was… I should've noticed this at Christmastime."

"I really hadn't noticed either. All of a sudden, he seems more forgetful." Glenora turned to Hank. "What about you?"

"He's been slipping a little at a time, I think. War tension takes its toll. But with what Roy knows best—all the things we do in the garage—he does all right." He went back into the dining room, and Henrietta hugged Glenora.

"Oh my, dear. You have so much to deal with here. I wish I'd been more alert."

"It's all right. What could you have done?"

An hour later, they emerged to a dining room set to rights, with Roy asleep beside the radio. Hank set down the newspaper and Glenora crossed the room to him.

"You worked some kind of magic here."

He shrugged, and Henrietta stepped in. "Why don't you two go out for a walk—it's turning into a beautiful day. I… I'd like to sit here with Roy until he wakes up, if you don't mind."

Glenora touched her dad's bony shoulder, and then Hank offered her his arm. "Come on."

They almost reached the door when he leaned down and swept up her hat. "Here, you ought to wear this in the Easter parade." Glenora turned, and he placed the simple straw creation atop her head.

His action was not lost on Henrietta, who swooned, "Oh my—you look elegant, Glenora."

Chapter Seven

"What a month March was, friends. To summarize, we liberated Manila, overwhelmed the Japanese in Burma, cleared the road to Rangoon, and started firebombing Japan, with heavy civilian casualties in Tokyo. Finland finally declared war on Germany, and the U.S. army took a strategic bridge over the Rhine—the Ludendorff, and the city of Cologne.

"Catch your breath—1945 has only begun, and V-2 rockets continue to hit Great Britain and Belgium. And let me remind you, all these actions come short of the fifteenth, the portentous Ides of March."

Roy switched off the radio and rose from his chair. Glenora, wearing her rose chenille bathrobe over her pajamas, bent over a shirt she was mending. "Sleep well, Dad."

No reply, but she was used to that. She focused on finishing the sock. But about ten minutes later, a crash upstairs shot her out of her chair. Her heart pulsed in her ears as she raced up the stairs.

"Dad..." Sprawled on the floor beside his bed with a bloody gash covering the side of his head, he made no sound.

She checked his breathing and nestled a clean wet towel

over the wound. But she couldn't rouse him. Better get Doc, although Dad would be furious with her.

Running through the side yard toward the Peterson's back porch, she breathed thanks that their light still shone, in spite of the heavy blackout drapes. Minor answered her pounding on the back door.

"It's Dad. He's fallen and needs Doc."

"I'll get him." Minor yelled back into the house. "Effie, hurry—go over to Glenora's while I run for Doc."

Glenora tore off for home, forgetting the Peterson's iron clothesline pole. She banged her forehead and stood there stunned, seeing more stars than the sky contained tonight. Laboriously, she gathered her senses and moved ahead again, a little slower this time.

When Doc came screeching up to the curb in his old Ford, she still felt woozy, and was glad Effie could lead Doc up the stairs. Minor and Doc carried Dad out to Doc's car on a stretcher, and when they passed Glenora, she tried to stand.

"Stay right where you are. Your dad's in good hands, but he may not come to tonight. Effie, you keep Glenora here, all right?"

Effie, about eighteen inches shorter than Glenora and tipping the scales at a possible one-hundred pounds, folded her arms across her chest and nodded. For the moment, Glenora allowed her to reign, but there was no way she wouldn't get to that hospital tonight.

The maelstrom in her head motivated her to let her sweet neighbor lady to fuss over her, but when the back door slammed over at Elsie's, both women jumped.

"I'm okay, really. Go on over and find out if Minor knows anything about Dad."

Elsie waffled, but Glenora focused on her eyes and stood up. "Please—maybe he can tell us something."

No sooner had the back door latched than she started out the front. A gulp of cool night air invigorated her, and she made her way through the side yard toward the pasture.

"I can do this. I can do this." From the first dilapidated automobile to the next, she staggered through the pasture. "Not going to fall. Nope." By the time the back of the garage came into sight, her breath came hard. If only Hank were still there—Dad said the other day he'd started spending part of his evenings working.

A faint light from the front gave her hope as she reached for the doorknob. Locked, of course. She rattled until the ancient hinges threatened to collapse, and just as she considered giving up, the door opened and she practically fell into Hank's arms.

"Oh... you're here. Thank goodness."

Hank switched on the light, and his expression altered from frustration to puzzlement. "Glen... what're you...?"

She clutched his arm, taking in the grease and oil smell that had become her daily lot. But right now, on Hank, any scent would do. "Hank, can you... would you take me to the hospital? Doc took Dad there, and..."

"Roy?" Genuine concern creased his brow. "Sure, jump in the truck."

He accompanied her up to the ward where Roy lay, quiet and pale. "Do you want me to stay?"

She shook her head. "I'll wait for Doc to come around and..."

Hank pulled a chair up to the bed for her. "I left the garage unlocked, but I'll be back. You've got quite a shiner developing. Don't try to walk home alone." His tone, steady and firm, sounded less like an order than a friendly reminder.

Thankful for the seat, Glenora fought an onslaught of dizziness. "All right."

Hank held Glenora's elbow descending the hospital steps. "Seems like we did this not so long ago."

"We did, and you learned to expect me to trip at the bottom."

"Not tonight, but that welt on your forehead is the size of a silver dollar. Did your dad fight you?"

Glenora's giggle was part exhaustion, part humor at the sight she must have made banging headlong into Effie's clothesline. "No, I couldn't rouse him at all. I sort of ran into a clothesline pole out back when I went to get help."

"Sort of? Hmm... my landlady's gone to a prayer meeting for the troops, so we'll stop by for some ice and you can rest on the porch a while."

"You only sit out there when she's gone?"

"Yeah. Otherwise, she talks my ears off. Anyway, she never gets home from that meeting before ten."

"You have kitchen privileges?"

Hank gave her a lop-sided grin. "In a manner of speaking."

The throb increased by the time he gave her a glimpse of his simple room when he grabbed a blanket. He retrieved some ice, set her in the porch swing, and dropped down beside her. Then he tucked her in, and Glenora simply let him.

"Seeing Dad so helpless unnerves me, you know?"

"Of course. Me too—but Doc seems to know what he's doing. Don't know how he can estimate how long Roy'll stay unconscious..."

"No."

Hank held the ice bag to her forehead without a word. After ten quiet minutes, except for the creak of the swing, he checked the time. "Almost nine-thirty, better get you home."

"Seems like it must be midnight."

Hank took the blanket inside. "Wait here while I get my car."

Feeling woozy was not Glenora's cup of tea, but a fine mist seemed awash inside her head. She focused on the word *tea*—just the ticket—Mama always believed a cup of strong tea worked wonders. Either that, or there'd be no sleep for her tonight. But weakness overcame her on the way home. Once inside, she slumped against the wall.

"Here, sit down."

"Some tea..." Her tongue played tricks on her, so Hank checked her pupils.

"They look normal, but maybe we should have Doc..."

That roused her, and she carefully enunciated. "A cup of tea is what I need... I'll be just fine."

"Mmm." Hank leaned her head onto the table and turned toward the cupboard.

"Second shelf on your left..." She drifted away to the sound of water running and the quick hint of gas as he turned on the burner and set the teapot to boil. Once again, she marveled at how quiet he was—no floorboard squeaks.

"All right, now. Come along with me." She let him half-carry her to the old stiff velvet couch, lift her legs, and cover her with Mama's afghan. "Going for some ice. Be right back."

She couldn't believe the pounding in her head, like Dad working on concrete with his sledgehammer. The next thing she knew, blessed coolness attended her pain, and Hank clinked Mama's china teapot lid.

Take yourself in hand. Can't let him keep waiting on you...

He helped her sit up, and the steaming drink did its magic. By the time Glenora finished her second cup and lay back against the cushions, her headache lessened a little. While Hank busied himself in the kitchen, she faded. The next thing she knew, moonlight doused the room.

In the corner, Hank's legs draped over the arm of the overstuffed chair, Mama's favorite. His head rested at an odd angle—he'd have a terrible crick in his neck by morning. Glenora tiptoed to the bathroom—her head felt so much better. Back on the couch, she slipped into sleep to the rhythm of Hank's soft breathing.

The next time she roused, sunshine blazed through the side windows, and out front, someone called to a child. Glenora took a slow walk to the kitchen, where her teacup had been washed and set back on the shelf. The clock ticked off the morning—she'd slept until nine o'clock, a first.

Still she had no inclination to hurry. Then she saw Hank's note on the table.

Hope you sleep a long time. I've handled a few enemy combatants in my time, so I can manage the garage today.

Mulling the idea of an entire day away from the shop, Glenora's next thought centered on Dad—better get over to the hospital. She opened the window to a wet world and springtime scents. Must've rained during the early hours. The promise of fertility filled the back yard when she stepped out on the porch steps.

Earth ready for tilling, a tractor put-putting in the distance, Minor raking his back yard, Mrs. Mosely puttering in hers. Simple small town life drenched in the hopefulness of spring.

"No better place to live, I say." That was Dad last summer, before they heard about Red's ship.

Then someone skipped up the steps with an envelope in hand. Glenora grasped the railing when she recognized Spencer, the Western Union man.

Apology filled his voice. "I tried at the garage, but your dad isn't there. Nothing to do but bring this over here."

He handed her an envelope and backtracked around the house. Glenora sank on the old butcher block Dad used for fileting fish, crushing the message that burned her fingers. How long she sat there, she had no idea. But suddenly, Hank squatted beside her, though she heard no footfall on the stairs. He calmly unbent her fingers and eased the envelope into his big hand.

"Want me to open this?"

She covered her face. "I don't want to know."

He opened the telegram, and she peeked through two fingers as he read.

"Mr. Roy Carson: Your son Ensign Victor Albert Carson hospitalized on AH-ll Refuge. Inquire Red Cross further information."

Glenora's stomach twisted, and Hank saw she couldn't take the news in. "Your brother's wounded, Glen. But he's *alive!*" She'd never seen his expression so animated. "He's on a hospital ship. Most likely, that means he'll be coming home."

Icy cold raked Glenora's shoulders and her throat hurt. "Do you think... should we tell..."

"Absolutely. If your Dad's conscious by now, this'll heal him overnight."

"But what if Red..."

"No 'what if's!'"

"Let me get my..."

"Yeah. I'll be at the garage. Left Uncle Slim in charge—for

once, I was glad he hung around." Hank's grin energized her.

"Ask him to stay a little longer, will you? If you don't mind going with me to tell Dad, that is."

He gave a little snort. "Sure. But remember, you're wearing that lovely pink robe—looks great on you, and I'm sure the nurse appreciated it last night. But I think people might start talking if you show up in it again today."

True to Hank's prophecy, the news about Red enlivened Dad, who awakened soon after they arrived. Within half an hour, he was ripping at his bandage.

A nurse entered with some porridge and coffee, but Roy shooed her away.

"Hate this place." He wrestled with his blanket, revealing a scrawny, hairy leg. When he tore at his bandage again, Hank grabbed his hand.

"Roy, I finally got Milford Fox's vehicle fixed last night, but it took twice as long without you. Come on, now—we need you at the garage. There's no other way to build up your strength but to eat."

In a sudden transformation, Roy's jaw relaxed. He stared at Glenora as if seeing her for the first time, then meekly opened his mouth.

Between bites, he asked, "Milford'll be off our backs now. Good. What's goin' on with the..."

"Patton's troops are almost to Mainz, Germany."

"Mainz? That'd be the Third Army's 80th Infantry Division."

"Yep. You sure do know your stuff."

Hank sent Glenora a sideways smile. "Won't be long now and we'll rout the Huns for good. With Patton trying to beat Monty to the Germans, who knows what'll happen?"

"Patton will win. Count on it."

Roy almost upset his bowl with a cheer, and Hank grinned. "I'd say he's back, Glenora. We'll have you in fine shape in no time, Roy."

Three days later he left the hospital without Doc's permission, and stayed home the next without arguing. When Glenora came home at noon, he'd started digging holes to plant potatoes.

He walked her back to the garage, where Hank hailed him. "Roy, you're lookin' awful spry."

Ten minutes later, Slim waltzed in.

"Heard you were under the weather. My niece on Minnie's side works at the hospital, you know. Was gonna stop in and visit you today."

"A fella can't even take a fall without the whole world knowin'." A snarl accompanied Roy's grumble, but the look Hank gave Glenora said it all.

Your dad's rediscovered a reason to wake up in the morning.

Elated with the word about Red, Glenora focused on trying to keep Dad from overdoing it. When she mentioned the need to get the garden planted before he did it himself, Hank offered to help.

"I'll be over right after supper. Used to help Aunt Minnie with her garden—good memories."

They worked until sunset, Hank turning soil and raking out lumps, Dad helping Glenora plant potatoes, onion sets, peas, and radishes. Then he went inside. Maybe he'd learned to take it a little easier. But as the last of daylight transformed into dusk, he made an announcement from the porch.

"Got some lemonade here. Glenora's cookies, too."

After they put the tools in the shed and washed up at the outdoor pump, Hank teased Glenora about the smudges on her face. He seemed so much like Tom that she splashed him with water, and he returned the favor. Then he lunged for her and she took off. He chased her around the house and caught her beside Mama's rose trellis.

In his arms, she caught her breath in the wonder of being held. His eyes glinted like sapphires in the shadows, but he kept his embrace light.

"Spray me in the face, will you?" She took in all the smells of her childhood, moist earth, growing things, and the evidence of hard work. Just as she sank deeper into his arms, the back door slammed and Dad called, "You two comin' in?"

Slowly, Hank released her. She tottered for a second, not wanting this to end—how long had it been since she'd laughed out loud? And then, feeling him so close...

Later, she lay awake, reliving that moment before Dad's voice interrupted what might have ended in a kiss. At least, it seemed Hank drew closer, and his hand on her back as they went up the porch steps told her he longed for nearness, maybe as much as she did.

A spring breeze fluttered the lace curtains Mama hung in her bedroom years ago, and a dog barked down the street. The memory of Joe Lundene kissing her under that same trellis never even crossed Glenora's mind.

Chapter Eight

"Nothing like hanging out clothes on a warm spring day." Mama might have stood beside Glenora, clipping wooden pins over wet clothes on the line that ran the length of the garden.

"Oh, Mama. I do miss you. So much has happened since you...You'd be so glad to know the war is almost over. And Red's alive—I can never stop giving thanks for that."

Sunshine warmed the back of her neck. Somewhere down the block, a dog barked, and she pictured Dad at work in the shop again, safe with Hank. He'd shown her kindness over and over, and here he was again, holding things together.

In the ensuing days, she'd wanted to ask him if he'd perhaps been a medic during the war, since he seemed so adept at first aid. But something held her back. No—if he wished to bring up the war, that would be different. He'd been so very kind to her and Dad, but she had no right to any part of his life he'd rather not revisit.

With the clothesbasket empty, she headed back inside. So nice to have extra time to do the washing this morning, knowing Hank could manage. But now she'd best get over to the garage and attend to the bills.

A couple of hours later, Slim danced through the door

and dove straight to where Hank's boots emerged from the cavernous underside of a farm truck. He hunched over and put his hands to his lips.

"The war's over, Hank. I'm telling you, the war's over." He waved several newspapers in his hand.

"Lookee here—bought every headline I could find. The Globe Gazette. The Courier..." He turned Glenora's way. "Take a look at this—EUROPEAN WAR ENDS. The Minneapolis Morning Tribune says so, too, the St. Paul Pioneer Press, the Rochester Post-Bulletin, and the Humboldt Republican."

Hank crawled off the floor, grabbed a paper and started to read. "Well, then. It's got to be true. Germany signs unconditional surrender..." He sank onto a stool and lost himself in the news.

Dad took one, too, and Slim brought the rest to Glenora. "Been waitin' so long... Gotta always remember this date, May the eighth." He stared from her to Hank, back and forth. Something struck him speechless, at last. Glenora immersed herself in the columns below the headline of the Tribune... could this really be true?

Finally, Slim ran back outside to inform more people, and Glenora let the news sink in. So yesterday's rumors amounted to more than hearsay. The radio report last night overflowed with the word *almost—almost certain, almost sure, we can almost say...* But now, actual evidence—these brazen headlines—filled her to bursting. She didn't know whether to laugh or cry, and once her shock dissipated, she raced around the counter to hug Dad. He hugged her back.

"Didn't know sometimes, Glen. But we made it. Now, we just gotta get Red back."

Across the room, Hank raised his head and studied them. The headline in his hands shouted, *VICTORY May 8, 1945*. With hardly a thought, Glenora ran to him, and he leaped up and crushed her in his arms. Then Dad was beating him on the back, and before long, the garage overflowed with exuberant men expressing their relief.

Someone announced they'd treat everyone to a beer at Leland's Tap or a root beer at the café, and they all trooped out, even Dad. All except Hank. Glenora's hand trembled so much, she couldn't attempt to do bookwork for a while. Hank stood before the truck, but made no move to pick up his wrench.

Finally, he crossed to the counter. "Doesn't seem right to go back to work yet, does it?"

She shook her head. When she leaned forward, he smoothed away her inadvertent tears and skirted the counter.

"Come here, Glenora." The light in his eyes made her whole body tingle as he swept her off her feet. "Can't do this right out here where the whole world can see."

The restrained power of his shoulder muscles sent a hungry wave through her. Easily the strongest man in town, he might also vie for the kindest—a parade of all he'd done for her father ran through her mind. Being carried made her feel so light, so carefree. Behind one of two big pillars holding up the roof, Hank stopped in the grimy shadows.

He took his time. Looked around. "There. This oughta do it." He set her down like a feather, drew her close, and took her breath away. Just as she'd imagined since that night under the trellis, nothing about this man disappointed her.

The notification came by mail. Victor Albert Carson had arrived at a recuperation center in Clinton the same day the headlines proclaimed victory in Europe. According to the letter, he'd stay there for an undetermined time before being released for home.

Glenora read the letter aloud to Roy, who stooped under an automobile hood in the garage. "Can you believe it? Red's in Iowa. We can go down on weekends to see him. Visiting hours from ten until three."

Later, over roast beef sandwiches, Hank made a proposal. "I can drive you down on Sunday if you like. Umm… how'd you make this beef taste so good?"

A month ago, when Effie offered a section of their new freezer for storage, Dad bought half a beef from Slim in anticipation of Red's return. Using Mama's reliable recipe, Glenora had slow roasted it. Dad rarely commented on her cooking, so Hank's compliment warmed her heart.

For one moment, she allowed for that old familiar image of teaching high school girls to cook and sew. She'd even promised Mama she'd finish college and use her talents in this way. But a moment of hindsight was more than enough. No use bemoaning lost opportunities—she never could have foreseen the war when she'd made that vow to Mama.

Meanwhile, she observed the mix of emotions playing over Dad's face. Maybe he'd rather wait 'til Red came home—there was no telling what shape he'd be in, and recent events had proven how much Dad despised hospitals. But in the end, he agreed.

"We've got some gas coupons—don't know if my old truck can make that long of a trip, though."

"My car can. With the speed limit now, it's probably a

five-hour trip down there. I'll pick you up at six o'clock."

With jitters in her stomach, Glenora followed Hank and Dad into the hospital. Who knew what to expect? This could turn out great, or seeing Red might send Dad into another slump. The long ride made walking a joy, and she dreaded the trip home, but Dad and Hank had never run out of things to discuss in the front seat.

An information clerk directed them to the activity room, where they paused outside the door and looked for Red through one of two windows.

"There he is—see, Dad? Over at that round table, the third man on the left side." Even from here, some scars showed on Red's face and hands, but he had all his limbs, unlike many of the men in the room.

Roy tried to speak but couldn't get a word to come out. Hank paused before grabbing the door handle. "Are you ready, then? I'll wait out here."

Glenora clutched Dad's forearm, and they walked through together. Heads turned, and the bright lights in the place made her blink.

"D'ya think we oughta...?" Second thoughts from Dad... but it was too late.

Red's face glowed when he spotted them, making his scars seem insignificant. He took his time getting out of his seat, but then half-ran into their arms. For a second, Glenora glanced back at the door, where Hank still watched. She gave him her best smile before turning her attention to Red.

"Well, I'll be jiggered. You came all this way—here, have

a cookie and some lemonade." Red played the host and led them to an eating area on the far side of the room.

"So good to see you, little brother." Glenora wiped her eyes with her hankie.

"Hey, no tears now. Look over there at that guy with no legs—I got off easy. What's a torn up face, anyhow?"

His comment freed Dad to start in about life in Halberton, Red coming back to work at the garage, and all the people looking forward to his return.

"Yeah. That'll be a grand day. Don't think I'll ever want to leave again."

Some more visitors arrived at the table, and the conversation multiplied. Soon, Dad was talking with them about their hometown, Nashua. Of course, they knew somebody he had met, and Glenora had a chance to talk with Red a little.

"Dad's lost a lot of weight. Has he been all right?"

"Well, he's had a couple of spells with his heart. Needs to slow down, Doc says. Might as well be honest—he's been in the hospital twice in the past few months."

"Mmm..."

"But seeing you is worth everything to him, Red, and when you come home..."

"You've been taking my place all this time, haven't you? Sure am grateful, sis."

She told him about Hank coming to help with all the work, and Red insisted on walking out to meet him.

When the visit was over, all Glenora could say was, "Oh Hank. It's really him. And he's going to be fine, I think. He seemed a little slow in his speech, but he said he's getting a lot of sleep and..."

As they drove north, Roy jabbered like a mockingbird.

"He can leave here in a few weeks. Said to tell Mary Ellen McWilliams to come see him—they was always sweet on each other. Think he's going to propose to her, Glen?"

In her own world in the back seat, Glenora let the question go.

"Hey, Glen—what do you think?"

"Yes, Dad." But what she really was thinking, she'd never tell a soul. Because she was thinking of Red coming home, marrying Mary Ellen, and... what...moving her into the house? He'd have to, since he had only his army pay saved up.

And then what? Glenora could scarcely put the questions together in her mind, much less verbalize them. She liked Mary Ellen, who would absolutely say yes—she'd waited for Red all this time and would do her best to make him happy.

That wasn't the real question. However hard Glenora tried, she simply couldn't picture living at home with Dad, Red, and Mary Ellen.

Seemed as though everyone had a plan for their life, but what about her?

About half way home, she dozed off, but woke when Hank pointed out a series of Burma Shave signs along the road.

Does your husband
Misbehave
Grunt and grumble
Rant and rave?
Shoot the brute
Some Burma-Shave

Your husband... Would she ever be able to claim that phrase? She'd never forget Hank's kiss the other day. Never. But he had shown no sign since then that it meant anything more than a whimsical end-of-the-war celebration. And yesterday, she overheard him say something to Dad about taking advantage of the G.I. Bill. But why hadn't he mentioned that to her?

Now they knew for sure that Red could take over in the garage. Hank said it looked to him as if military protocol probably was keeping him in the hospital. The future looked bright for him, and for Hank, too—he'd helped Dad out during a rough time, and now he'd move on.

Glenora leaned her head back as they turned onto the last bumpy thirty-mile strip of graded road used by the Red Ball Transportation Company on their route from Waverly to Charles City. Dad still chattered away in the front seat.

"D'ja hear 'bout them trucks they call Red Ball Express over in France? Wonder if somebody from around here gave 'em the name."

"I think the red ball comes from the flag they bring out to announce a Vice-Admiral's ship, Roy. Means something important's coming. The railroad uses a red ball, too, for perishable loads that need priority shipping."

Hank almost never discussed the war, though the talk in the shop focused on it every day. Now, Glenora strained to hear what he was saying. "We couldn't have won without those supply trucks, that's for sure. I heard when they were feeding Patton's army, almost a hundred and fifty trucks crossed France at night—lots of black men among those drivers, too."

"Is that so? I seen some of 'em over in France when I was there. Ain't that Red Ball what they call the thirty-fourth out of Minnesota, too? The Kyle boy was with 'em, I'm pretty sure."

"That's right. Those units have had it rough—almost non-stop fighting in North Africa and up through Italy and France. Four long years of it—they just got finished with one battle and headed into another. Don't know if I could've taken it that long."

Glenora strained her ears even harder.

"Pretty rough, eh?"

After a long pause, Hank finally replied. "Yeah."

A snore told Glenora Dad had finally dropped off to sleep, but there was no use trying to have a conversation with Hank. The gravel under the wheels created a roar that took over the car.

Fields of corn, oats, and soybeans flew by, and she thought about Red's return. She'd have to plan a party—let's see, she could bake up a storm and Effie would be excited to help. Maybe Minor would make a batch of his wonderful home-made ice cream.

Outside St. Ansgar, huge onion fields exuded the intense scent of growing plants. When she looked up, Hank caught her gaze in the rear-view mirror. He had to concentrate on driving, of course, but the high color in his cheeks declared he'd been watching her. Was he sending some message her way?

Usually their silent communications centered on her dad, but seeing Red had done wonders for him. She knew Dad would cooperate with Doc's instructions now, knowing Red would soon be home. She looked away, but Hank's steady gaze drew her back again. The trouble was, she had no idea what those big eyes were trying to tell her.

With Dad on a calmer course and full summer here, Glenora spent more time in the garden. Evenings found her squatting between rows to nurture her fledgling plants, and something about having her hands in the soil quieted an inner sneer that troubled her on her walks home after work.

You face a lonely, solitary life. No doubt about it, you'll become an old maid.

She'd never really minded being alone, though. In fact, she treasured serene times by herself after Mama died, with Dad ensconced before the radio and Red over at Mary Ellen's every evening. Back then, she had taken long walks down by the river, often reading until the sun set and meandering home in her own time.

In high school, she'd watched couples form and break up, but until Joe chose her, she hadn't made finding a husband a priority. Plenty of time ahead for that kind of thing, so she put her mind to her studies. Joe's attention made her feel special, yet she'd still planned to become a teacher.

But then the war changed everything. A hoard of local boys left in a hurry, and now a good share of them had returned home—every day, parents, girlfriends, and wives waited at the small train depot down the street, hoping their loved one would jump off the train. Seemed like smooching young couples inhabited every corner of Halberton, and wedding bells filled the air.

While she celebrated with them, Glenora couldn't help but consider her own situation. Where was her sailor? Gone forever. Would another man ever choose her? Her fantasies about Hank appeared unlikely now—obviously, he had dreams of his own to pursue.

A cooling June breeze reached the back yard, and next

door, Effie and Minor spoke in low tones, tending their own garden. Their patience with each other through the years wove a tale of true devotion, especially when Minor veered from the straight and narrow a time or two.

If only Mama had lived longer—a tide of hurt burned the backs of Glenora's eyes. Mama missed her graduation, now she would not be here for Red's homecoming, and soon, she'd miss his wedding and all the joys of being a grandparent.

Early on in life, when Grandma died, Glenora accepted that sorrow touched everyone, but as twilight encroached, her sense of loss seemed relentless. If Mama had lived, they'd be working out here together this evening. They'd be cooking and baking together and making strawberry preserves in a week or so.

True, nothing stayed the same, but an ocean of change inundated her right now. Only one thing to do: endure the troubles life brought and wait for them to pass—the same way she'd made it through the war so far.

Sometimes in the night, she recalled times when she'd been at odds with Mama. For some reason, she'd always felt an easier connection with Dad and often went to him with problems rather than to her mother. Red, on the other hand, tended to spend more time with Mama, and when he first showed an interest in working at the shop, Dad had seemed surprised.

A gentle rising wind carried away her whisper. "You never let on, Mama, but if I hurt you, I'm sorry."

In the living room, Dad turned the radio up midway through the news, and afterward, Edythe Wright crooned "The Music Goes 'Round and Round" to Tommy Dorsey's orchestra background. How Mama loved that song!

When Glenora stood up, her left knee popped. After stretching her back, she carried her weed basket to the burn pile. Never any let-up to the plantain and dandelions—they would continue to invade until the first hard frost. And as always, tenacious smartweed did its best to make life difficult for the peas and carrots.

Maybe that was the way of the world in general, even when no war complicated things. You had to take the bad with the good and keep doing your best. That's what Grandma used to say—take the bad with the good.

Before heading up the back steps, Glenora scraped her garden shoes on the iron scraper and surveyed the western sky. A glorious mix of hues made quite the show, from deep orange to scarlet to several shades of magenta, purple and violet. Finally, a line of gold encroached until at last, gray-blue took over the horizon.

In spite of her dim prospects, she fixed her thoughts on the one shred of hope that had come to her this week—an ad in the county paper. She knew how to keep books and do accounting, and that's what some business in Osage needed.

The idea of sneaking behind Dad's back bothered her, but she mustn't let him know until Red came back. Maybe after his wedding. With him ensconced before the radio, she washed up and headed for her room. No reason she couldn't apply.

Chapter Nine

When Glenora started doing books on this early July morning, Hank still hadn't arrived, and Dad seemed unconcerned. An hour later, three new work orders had piled up, but no Hank. Dad bustled about like nobody's business, so Glenora kept at her work until somebody came in and asked where Hank was. She could only shrug.

"Ask Dad—maybe he knows." She had an inkling he did, but for some reason, had kept the information from her. Of course, she wondered, but an inner voice said, *That's all right. You may as well get used to this.*

Crossing the street for the mail, she cast a glance toward Hank's boarding house down the street. No! She shook herself—he had his own life, and his comings and goings were clearly none of her business. He'd been kind to her, true, but she mustn't read anything more into that.

Piling the usual bills into her leather satchel, she slammed the Carson Garage post office box a little harder than normal. Mrs. Hastings, who worked for the bank, caught her eye, and Glenora put on a friendly smile.

"We hear Red's coming home soon—everyone's so thrilled for you."

"Yes, we got to see him last week. Thanks."

A surge of heat flashed through Glenora. This is what every single person she met today was going to say. She didn't mind...but maybe she'd take a short walk on her old route. Dad seemed just fine these days, and ought to be able to manage. Then she'd go fix lunch, which would give her another twenty minutes away from the garage.

Through the alley beside the post office, she fled. Yes, fled—she needed an escape. Beyond the next block, open country beckoned her. Even ten minutes out here would do her good.

Soon she was running, running...toward the river, toward the shelter of those high cottonwoods, toward...

Toward what? It was one of those times words failed her. Panting, she sprawled under a cottonwood and leaned back against its solid trunk. Reliable, trustworthy...always here when she came. A few deep breaths, and she opened her eyes to the glories around her. In winter, whites and blacks and deep browns drew sketches on the riverbank. Today, every imaginable shade of green painted undeniable beauty.

A few feet away, some unruly weeds stirred. Glenora fixed her eyes on the spot, and sure enough, some dark brown fur showed. She wiggled her foot, and the small, furry blob moved a few inches. Hopped. A baby bunny, like the ones she'd found as a child while Dad and Tom fished.

The thought of Tom brought a question. Why didn't he check in on Dad once in a while? True, he had his own family and a heavier workload the past few years, with so many Hormel workers off to war. When Mama had been ill, he visited a few times, but after her funeral, they rarely heard from him.

Now that she considered it, she couldn't recall hearing

from him all spring. Aunt Henrietta knew about Dad's spell, so she figured the word got passed to Tom. But maybe not. Was *that* her responsibility, too?

Now, now—feeling sorry for yourself again?

With her momentary tranquility dashed by the tussle in her mind, Glenora opened the mail satchel with a sigh. Thumbed through the letters—lots of work here. At least one payment was enclosed, for the motorcycle repairs. That made sense. Howard Turney could rely on his monthly government check for his war board duties.

The last envelope produced a wave of expectation—the Daylight Store, one of Osage's finest. That's where she'd sent her application, and here lay the reply. Aware of her flightiness today, she almost cast the letter back into the satchel. Not a good time for another disappointment.

But curiosity overcame her, and she read the brief note. Then she read it again aloud:

Dear Miss Carson,

Thank you for your kind reply to our advertisement in the Mitchell County Press. Your qualifications fit our job description perfectly, and we would like to speak with you further. Would it be possible for you to come for an interview the morning of July second?

We hope to hear from you soon.

Ezra Daylight
Proprietor

Fresh energy flowed through Glenora. She held the letter close for a few seconds before stuffing it back into the satchel. She'd been accepted—they wanted to interview her! It wasn't teaching, but still...

By the time she reached home, perspiration sat in the hollow of her back. She washed up and quickly made sandwiches. Mustn't let Dad know about this, but she could take the train down to Osage on the second—a Monday. She'd figure out some excuse, and hopefully Hank would still be around then.

If he has nothing better to do...

"My goodness, Glenora, you're certainly touchy today. For all you know, he's sick—deathly ill." The chastisement came from her own mouth, but Mama might have said it. Yes, she'd been too judgmental, too self-centered.

Well, better get on with the rest of the day. She hefted the satchel over her shoulder and grabbed a bag with their lunch—hers and dad's. A glance back over the yard showed the garden looking even better than last year's, poised to produce a bumper crop. That meant a load of work ahead for her, but at least it was work she enjoyed. She hoped Mary Ellen liked cooking, baking and the gardening that came with living here.

Working for the Daylight Store would mean she'd need to find an apartment in Osage and start a whole new life. Moving out of this house with so many memories of Mama would be bittersweet, but the new life part tantalized her.

When she passed through the work area, Hank's enormous feet stuck out under a car. He probably ate lunch somewhere else, but it wasn't her problem if he hadn't. Dad had a sandwich and so did she—that's what she'd focus on from now on—family—and her upcoming interview.

"I'm taking the train down to Osage on Monday. Will you be here for sure?"

About to walk out for the day, Hank turned back with raised eyebrows. "Sure." He hesitated as though he wanted to say more, but after giving Glenora a searching look, he continued out. Elbows on the counter, she supported her chin with her fists. Since she hadn't started a conversation with him for days, of course he'd been surprised. But yesterday he'd been gone again, without a word from him about his whereabouts.

As usual, she told herself his business had nothing to do with her, and rewarded Hank with silence. She'd taken to wolfing down her sandwich at home rather than eating with him and Dad—too much tension in the air.

But still, she wondered what it was like to have a dream and be able to pursue it. More than once, she'd stifled a question like, "Hank, tell me about Iowa State, would you? Have you signed up for classes yet?"

With the G.I. Bill made into law over a year ago, she also wanted to ask why he'd waited so long. Had he decided to stay here because of Dad's health, until Red arrived? He could have been well on his way to earning his degree—at least he'd told her that much. Before they stopped talking, that is.

Ever since the last time he failed to show up for work, Hank had turned extra quiet. She'd kept bringing enough lunch for him, but often, he left in the middle of the day for a half hour instead of eating with Dad.

Once again, she reminded herself of a simple fact: she had no right to know anything about his plans. Better concentrate on her own—that evening, she pulled out the suit she'd bought last fall with Aunt Henrietta. Yes, this rose blouse would be perfect for the interview. Businesslike, but chic. Too warm to wear the jacket outdoors, but she could put it on just before she walked into the Daylight Store, which as she recalled, was kept cool somehow.

To boost her confidence, she wore the outfit to church. A total of four compliments convinced her of the decision, and this excursion also provided practice walking in her black pumps. Early Monday morning, she dressed and hurried to the train station.

At a brief stop in a small town to take on more passengers, the jitters started. After all, she'd never been interviewed before. Never had a job outside the garage. She chuckled, thinking of Dad asking to interview her for that one.

Stepping out at the depot, she faced north, clutching the beautiful leather purse she rarely carried. To her right lay Main Street, and even though she had a full forty-five minutes to pass, she started out past the Osage theater, where *And Then There Were None* was playing. Someone told her the murder mystery scared the socks off them—but she forgot who.

Ah, well. The array of businesses here stirred something in Glenora as she passed—George Birum's Buick Garage, Davidson's Electric, the Kane Drugstore, Karwac's Bakery, Chapman's Grocery, and Eddie Tesch's Snack Shop with signs offering hamburgers and malts. McGrane's Clothing—must be a competitor of the Daylight Store—Pohle's Drugstore, Gillises Grocery, and Champion's Furniture Store.

A quick detour into the Cleveland Hotel to admire the relaxing atmosphere—Mama told her a family from New York had built it. Then she passed another grocery, and Scott's Store—surely another competitor for Mr. Daylight. A few buildings down, the Clover Farm Grocery sent out a mix of scents, including fresh-butchered meat. Beyond Lashton's Drugstore came the Daylight Store. Glenora had been inside a few times, and in Art's Shoes down the street, to prepare for school every fall.

Still fifteen minutes early, she entered and strolled the aisles as a customer might. A lady purchased something, so the clerk put her money in a transparent canister and sent it up a tube toward a balcony. There, a white haired woman took out the money, made change, wrote something down, and sent the change back in the canister.

In the meantime, the clerk wrapped the customer's purchase and when the canister arrived, counted out her change. Watching the transaction eased Glenora's fears—now she knew how the store's daily transactions worked. She followed the signs to the basement and lost herself in advertisements for new electric irons, modern toasters, and an electric mixer.

After checking her watch, she climbed back to the main floor, where a middle-aged man met her and introduced himself. Mr. Daylight. He led her up the second flight of stairs to an office and motioned for her to take a chair near his desk. From the moment she sat down across from him, serenity filled her—chatting here came easier than dealing with curmudgeonly farmers.

Mr. Daylight showed her around the store and introduced her to three workers. Back at his office, he shook her hand. "My son Allan co-manages the store with me, and we'll make a decision about this position within the next few weeks. Either way, you can expect to hear from us."

A few weeks... Glenora left the store feeling as though that were forever. But Red's wedding was only two weeks away, and she'd be knee deep in preparations. All would be well.

Once again, the War Bond banner Glenora had worked on more than four years ago swung high over the school gymnasium. Nobody could say they hadn't gotten their mileage out of that creation—here it was, August sixth, 1945, and no one had mentioned replacing the huge fabric swatch that appeared at every fundraiser.

Back in home economics class, the girls in her class made the sewing machine hum after days stitching the hems and words that proclaimed the community's patriotism:

WE OFFER ALL WE CAN FOR OUR BOYS.

Joe had perished a few months before, and plenty of tears fell on that fabric as Glenora sewed.

Yes, and that had become the town's motto. Over and over, people gave what they could, donated what they could, and then dug into their pockets a bit deeper. This afternoon, workers milled around the polished oak floor, preparing for tonight's dance. At the church food booth, nonstop chatter filled the air when she delivered three dozen raisin cookies and an apple pie.

Effie gushed over that pie. "Oh, my goodness, Glenora. If you aren't the best baker in town, I don't know who is."

"I don't get the time to do this very often lately. Sure seemed good to work with pastry dough again."

"You work such long hours—hopefully when Red and Mary Ellen get married, you'll get to stay home more. You and Mary Ellen will get along just fine, don't you think? And before we know it, there'll be children's voices in your back yard."

Thankfully, Effie turned to two other women making sandwiches. "Just think, this might be our last fundraiser, girls. Surely Japan will surrender soon, especially after that bombing today—what was the name of that city again?"

"Hiroshima. I would certainly think so. Did you hear that the pilot who dropped the bomb named his plane after his mother?"

"You don't say? Well, all I care about is getting our boys back home."

"Yes, but we're not out of the woods yet, even in Europe. Yesterday, Walt Hendricks' mother got a letter from him—he's in Germany. They're seeing things there that we'd never believe—horrible camps for Jewish people and places where thousands of innocent citizens who hated the Reich were killed."

Another woman added, "A lot of our boys are still in danger in the Pacific, especially on remote islands where the enemy hides out. I suppose it'll take a while, once the Japs surrender, for word to reach everyone."

"Then there's the hospital ships—oh, those poor nurses working night and day. I can't even imagine what they're going through." Effie gave a heartfelt sigh. "But still, things are better now—bound to be. The armistice has been signed with Germany, and surely, Japan..."

The bouncy beat of a new song...a crooner asking to be kissed once, twice, and once again...came over a radio someone had stationed on a small table near the entrance. Effie swung her hips, and some of the other ladies joined in on the chorus.

Glenora walked over to the Baptist church ladies' booth. If she hadn't felt so glum, she might have done some dancing, too, even if most of the women here ignored the music and would never have swung their hips. But one younger woman who graduated a few years ahead of her motioned her closer.

"I love that new song Kitty Kallen sings. My Grandma

remembers waiting for her sweetheart, Grandpa Elliot, after the Great War. She still hums *As Time Goes By*. She says they thought back then that the war would never end, but then it did. Hard to believe that now we've survived another one."

Mabel Kline chimed in. "My John got so sick on the troop ship back then, he swore he'd never leave Iowa again."

Glenora declined to add anything. She loved the beat of this song, but every time it played, the references to kissing made her wince. With their wedding so close, Red and Mary Ellen kissed each other all the time—luckily, they spent most evenings outdoors or at Mary Ellen's house. But just about everybody else around town seemed to be hugging. Cynthia's brother had returned already, along with Tillie's husband. Kissing everywhere.

If only Mr. Daylight would hurry up and write. The interview replayed in her mind so often, she had the dialogue memorized. None of his questions troubled her, and he'd voiced agreement with most of her answers. He'd given her no timeline for hiring a new worker, but she had expected a letter for two weeks now.

Every day Hank's absence troubled her, like the giant hole ripped in the garage sign, still unfixed. He'd left so suddenly—and without a word to her. He and Red got along fine, but Hank kept dropping hints about going to Iowa State in the fall. And then, just like that, he left last week.

Something sour rode Glenora's throat these days, and she turned from the church ladies to swallow it down. She must regain her equilibrium. It wasn't that Hank hid anything from her. In July, he told her and Dad he'd be going, just before Red came home.

He stayed until Red picked up the routine at the

garage—he wouldn't have had to. Glenora shook herself. *You've dealt with losing someone before—it's not as if Hank died.* But just when she'd been so hopeful he wanted her in his life, everything fell apart.

Had all they shared meant nothing to him? Had what she'd seen as his silent communication with her been only her imagination? She strong-armed herself each morning, determined to stay cheerful, but by noon, her misery returned.

Fall already showed signs in the big maples out back, turning leaves golden little by little. Her favorite season, but each day, she dragged herself out of bed. Every time a car drove by, she checked to see if by some miracle, Hank had returned.

At the same time, she couldn't be happier for him. He deserved his education, and nearly died for this opportunity. She must rise to the occasion and overcome the self-pity that threatened her every waking moment. The thing was, this turn of events brought her scholarship to mind—that golden opportunity she'd given up years ago. For Red. For Dad.

When evening came, she felt far older than her years—one fourth of her lifetime gone, and the last four and a half years stolen by the war. If she'd been able to serve in the forces, it might be different. The WACS, even some women who'd joined the Marines, could come back from the war excited about life in little Halberton, Iowa.

But she'd stayed right here, doing her duty, as Mama would have wanted. There really had been no choice. She couldn't have left Dad alone with all the shop work and worries. No, loyalty kept her here, but now that same loyalty angered her. She returned to help Effie create perfect rows of pie and cookies and cake on trays lined with towels. That job complete, she decided she could do more good back home.

"I'll be back later, Effie." *Probably.* On her way out, Glenora caught her toe on a chair, and the crashing sound it made against the cement wall brought her some satisfaction.

In the kitchen, she made some tea and stared out at the back yard. Might as well work in the garden. Somebody had to do it, and nobody else volunteered. She pulled on an old pair of worn dungarees, tied a bandana around her hair, and carried another cup of tea to the porch. Maybe sitting here in the late afternoon sun would help.

The more she thought about it, the less she wanted to attend the fundraising dance. Red and Mary Ellen would be there, kicking up a storm, and so would John and Tillie, plus every other couple madly in love.

The sharp aroma of Mama's favorite green tea had a soothing effect, just what she needed. She set her cup down and moseyed out to the green bean rows, still producing far too much for this small family. Twenty minutes later, she'd filled a three-gallon pail. Only half done.

Mrs. Mosely poked around next door, so Glenora called her over. "Do you need any beans?"

"Why sure, I could use some. The blight got mine something terrible." Their diminutive neighbor opened wide her apron and Glenora scooped it full.

"There'll be more in a few days—come on over and help yourself."

"Bet you're all excited, with the wedding so close." Mrs. Mosely lowered her voice as though somebody might hear. "Been working on a cross-stitch towel set for the newlyweds. I sure hope they like it."

"Oh, that's so nice of you. I'm sure they will."

"Well, I'm off to get these ready for canning—hate to do

it tomorrow, though. Do you think it'd be all right to wait 'til Monday, if I keep them cool in the basement?"

Glenora nodded. "Then you can pick the patch again on Tuesday."

Mrs. Mosely retreated, and so did Glenora's temporary reprieve from pondering what happened between her and Hank. Or failed to happen. A mourning dove sent forth its lonesome evening cry, and she sank down at the edge of the garden.

Gotta get myself out of this slump. Can't go on like this much longer.

Then the ad she'd seen in the paper replayed in her mind. "Needed: bookkeeper for busy department store, plus other duties. Mr. Daylight had explained what those duties were. "Miss Hanson will retire in the next couple of years, so you'd also take over her work up in the balcony. Until then, we'd have you clerking, too. What department would interest you most?"

That was easy. "Oh, the kitchen goods downstairs, sir." His pleased expression came back to her today, and she pictured herself explaining the ins and outs of a new small appliance to a customer. Not what she'd set her heart on, but at least it would be a change.

Maybe she could start the first of October, after Dad was used to Mary Ellen living here. Besides knowing how to cook and clean and sew, Mary Ellen seemed perfect for taking care of the garage accounts. She'd probably jump at the chance—anything to spend more time near Red.

The hot tea fortified Glenora. The tomatoes needed picking, too, and why not pull the beets while she was at it? All the while, her desire to avoid the dance strengthened.

Chapter Ten

"Couldn't be a nicer day for a wedding. Mary Ellen and Red look absolutely perfect for each other. It's so wonderful he came home, Glenora, after all you and your dad have gone through. Sure do wish your mother could be here to enjoy it, though. I still miss her so much."

"Me too. Yes, you're right, Effie. Mary Ellen's a peach."

Glenora's new sister-in-law bobbed her head at the well-wishers who threw rice on the happy couple outside the church. Glenora strained to see if the last minute stitching she performed on Mary Ellen's lovely gold suit showed. Just two hours before the ceremony, Mary Ellen came to her distressed.

"Don't know how this seam came out. I've tried it on a few times, but not since May, I guess. Do you think I've gained weight? Today it looks like it could burst at the hip any moment. I could fix it, I'm sure, but I'm so nervous. Could you help me out, Glen?"

Glenora pulled out Mama's old machine and greased the treadle. It seemed only natural for Mary Ellen to call her what Red and Dad did. "Of course. There's nothing I wouldn't do for you today, Mary Ellen."

Now, the brilliant burgundy maples in front of the church spread a carpet along the sidewalk for Red and Mary Ellen, off on a three-day honeymoon to visit Red's army buddy and his wife in Omaha, Nebraska. With a boutonniere in his pinstriped suit jacket, Red beamed at the crowd gathered outside the church.

Dad grinned from ear to ear as people shook his hand and congratulated him on his lovely new daughter-in-law. Slim and Minnie, the Petersons, Mrs. Mosely, and scads of other townsfolk attended, although Red and Mary Ellen had planned the simplest of ceremonies.

Of course, Tom brought his family, and was busy catching up with old friends and relatives. Gerold drove over, too, and Aunt Henrietta was in her glory. In the basement, Glenora looked up from helping in the kitchen, and spotted her glamorous hat, matching suit and gloves.

Her aunt waved and hurried over. "What are you doing back here? You should be out there enjoying the guests. Oh, I wish we could go shopping again this trip, but I need to get right back."

"Looks like you've already been there—you're spectacular in that new suit."

"You're a picture in yours, honey. This burgundy would look good on you too—any rich, deep shade. Maybe we can spend a day together at Thanksgiving."

Glenora swallowed a ripple of disappointment. She'd wanted to share about her interview—Aunt Henrietta could keep a secret. Oh, well, she'd write her a letter.

Aunt Henrietta tiptoed to whisper one last thing in her ear. "Where's that wonderful fellow who was working at the garage last spring? Sure seemed to me like he had eyes for you."

Glenora groaned inwardly, and a shrug was all she could manage. Luckily, someone tapped Henrietta on the arm and she turned. Their snippets of conversation floated by like autumn leaves.

"So nice to see all these weddings taking place."

"Glad our young people can get a new start and make up for lost time."

"My cousin's son came back in July and married his sweetheart the next day—wonderful, isn't it?"

Up in the sanctuary, Glenora removed wide white ribbon bows from the pews. If only she could remove her feelings for Hank so easily. Feeling sadder by the moment, she lugged two tall vases of dahlias home. Then she trekked back, aware of people still milling about in front of the church.

It's not that I'm not happy for Red...I am. It's just that I feel so...

The sanctuary, still as stone, beckoned her to stay a while, so she took a seat in the third pew from the back, where late afternoon sunlight shimmered on the back of the oak pew. Such beautiful grain in these seats, all hand-tooled by Effie's grandfather two generations ago. She'd miss this place, so close to home, and always so welcoming. Sometimes after Mama died, she'd slip in for a few moments on her way from the post office, and serenity never failed to find her here.

But today, that sense of all being well in spite of the reality she faced eluded her. An old maid...she'd never had grand visions of romance, but after Joe, she did still expect to become a wife and mother someday.

A shaft of bitterness ran the length of her backbone. And then Hank had to show up. Why couldn't Slim have asked somebody besides Dad to take him under his wing? Why didn't Hank go back to wherever he called home after the war, anyhow?

Knowing the only path to peace was getting this out of her system, she closed her eyes and cried, "Why would he lead me on and then leave? I just don't understand!"

Her voice echoed the quiet space, but no answer occurred to her. No, only muted chatter from the basement where husbands and wives, engaged couples, and her little brother and his bride made merry. She rested her head on the pew, cool and smooth.

All the lessons she'd learned here, downstairs at Sunday school, and at Mama's knee escaped her right now. Dark thoughts overwhelmed her. *Help me...please help me. I can't shake this alone.*

Finally, snippets of a familiar hymn—one of Mama's favorites—cascaded through her thoughts...*But we never can prove the delights of His love, until all on the altar we lay...the joy He bestows...*

As on that morning when she'd been hanging out the clothes, Mama seemed very near. *Trust and obey...* she would say, "Being happy is a choice, Nora."

Glenora straightened her shoulders and set her mind, but her feelings refused to follow along. The image of Hank's face—that scarred face she'd come to love—rose before her. She studied the altar. "Help me to leave him here, Lord. I know these feelings will fade eventually."

She set a couple of dahlia vases on wooden stands for tomorrow's church service, loaded the last of the decoration boxes into her arms, and headed down the narrow back stairway. But even the glorious fall sunshine failed to cheer her.

Back at home, she put off going back to the church to say

good-bye to Aunt Henrietta and the others. They probably wouldn't miss her anyway. But then, she remembered the shears she'd set in a back corner of the vestry after she and Mary Ellen arranged the flowers this morning. Mama's best pair—couldn't leave them at the church all night.

Using the shortcut through the lot, she heard something in the back of the garage when she passed. Strange. She paused to listen. There it was again, some sort of sliding and clinking.

No good peering through the back window, since Red had piled boxes of parts there. With the war mostly over and what was left of her generation reclaiming their places, several people had bought new cars, so the amount of repairs increased by the day. Red instituted a new process: why not order in the most common parts, so they'd be able to service vehicles quicker? Otherwise, he said, someone might start up a new garage and compete with them.

Dad agreed, and Red did the ordering and stacking, leaving only a narrow walkway in the back room. Glenora worked hard to keep track of the orders and make sure they were paid on time.

So far, no one had mentioned Mary Ellen's role, but it was only a matter of time. By then, Glenora's secret plan would surely come to fruition. Mr. Daylight had mentioned an October first starting date. Quietly, she prepared for her move up in her room at home, throwing out non-essentials and sewing up a couple of new outfits in the evenings.

She swallowed down her distaste at the idea of sitting in an office all the time, doing paperwork at her boss's bidding. Ah well...she ought to be glad for a job, and maybe she'd be such a good clerk that Mr. Daylight would give her some hours in the basement every day.

Although Red would never say so, she bet he and Mary Ellen would sigh with relief when she moved out. Surely they'd rather have the upstairs to themselves, now that Dad was moving to the downstairs bedroom.

And for an old maid, any old room in a boarding house would do. That bitter tide of emotion ranged through Glenora's chest again. She batted back tears and grasped for the words from Mama's hymn.

Still, she decided to wait to tell Dad. Too much change too fast. In a couple of weeks, he'd be used to Mary Ellen's cooking. Then one night, she'd ask him to take her for a ride, show him the store in Osage and her new place of residence, tell him she needed to start a new life, but she'd still be close if he needed anything.

Another sound came from inside the garage, so she tried the back door and found it unlocked. Odd—what could be going on?

Skulking like a criminal, she advanced through the storage area. When someone moved one of the stools up front, she froze in place. Then a drawer opened behind the counter. She grabbed the closest weapon she could find, an old rusty crowbar, and crept into the service area.

A few steps, then a few more, and she stopped to look around. So far, nothing seemed out of order. The stools never stayed in the same place anyway, but what was that swishing sound from behind the counter? She could swear another drawer slid open or shut.

Goosebumps ran the length of her arms. A pity to have endured the troubles of war and secured the promise of a new job, only to perish in a robbery right here in the garage.

For a full minute, silence reigned. She didn't know whether

to stay put or move forward. Then someone caught her from behind, sending her heartbeat into a wild spin. A large warm hand wiggled the crowbar from her grip.

"Better be careful. You might hurt someone with this."

Serious dark eyes met hers. Serious, but laughing at the same time.

"Hank?"

"Who'd you think?"

"Well, I... I didn't know you still had a key."

"Yes, but there's another key I'm looking for, Glenora Carson." His tone, playful yet somber, intrigued her.

What other key could he want? Only two words occurred to her—a question. "You're back?"

Hank sat down on a stool and crossed his arms. "Not exactly, but I didn't want to miss Red's wedding. Guess I expected you'd think I'd come."

"But I didn't see you in the congregation."

"I lurked in the shadows up in the balcony, where I could have a birds' eye view of you standing up for Red and Mary Ellen. But when they walked down the aisle together, you slipped down the back way..."

Glenora bristled. "I had to make sure the kitchen ladies had everything ready down in the basement."

"And when I went down there for some cake, you..."

This conversation was getting her riled. "I had to make sure everything got put away up in the sanctuary."

"Umm...makes sense. Always taking care of things for everybody."

What could she say? He'd just described her lot in life.

After a long silence, Hank spoke again. "But when you leave, they'll all have to take care of themselves."

"What?" A sharp edge entered her voice. She'd been so careful—how could he have discovered her plan?

His expression gave her no clues. He set the crowbar down on a workbench and pulled up a stool, resting one foot on his other knee. "At least, I hope you're going to leave." He searched her face. "What I mean is... I stopped in here to search for something, but since you're here..." His face flushed a rosy shade. "Roy sent me over here to look for the letter about your scholarship."

"What?" He was talking nonsense—she flailed for words. "That was issued so long ago, it's no good now. And what does Dad know about my things? Why would I bring that letter over here?"

"I don't know. But I'm not so sure the scholarship's no good." Hank paused to peer at her. Then he shrugged. "Anyway, your dad couldn't find it at the house. Said he looked everywhere when you went to Osage one day. You do still have those papers from Iowa State, don't you?"

"I... yes." She visualized the worthless sheets of paper, tucked away with Joe's letters and all the rest of her hopes for a bright future. Her irritation increased—why should Hank care, anyway? She attempted to analyze the odd rise of his right eyebrow, but it told her nothing.

"Well, I've done some checking down at the college, and just in case we don't find it, they still have a copy in their records."

She almost asked, "So what?"

"There's a good chance that, because of the war turning people's lives upside down, they might still make good on it."

The garage swirled around her—barrels, tires, broken-down vehicles, tools... What could all of this mean?

"But I just…"

"Just what?"

"Gave it all up."

"What do you mean by *it all?*"

"Everything. My dreams, my hopes…"

"So you'd rather not study down there?"

"Why, I… no. Of course I'd love to, but actually I gave that up way back when Mama died—somebody had to keep things running at the house."

Hank angled his head, and the tenderness in his tone made her retreat a step. "Mustn't ever do that, Glenora—give up on things. That's one thing the war taught me. As long as we're still alive, there's always hope."

Suddenly she remembered the key he'd mentioned, and tore her eyes away from him. "You… you were looking for a key?"

"Oh, that." Hank cleared his throat. "I was referring to the key to your heart. Whether or not the college honors that scholarship, I want you to come to Iowa State with me. I've already got our name on the list for married student housing for the second semester."

Our name… married student housing… She thought she'd never catch her breath.

"Mar…?"

"You can't live in married student housing unless you're married." The twinkle in his eyes made her bite her lip.

"Stop it. What do you mean?"

He rubbed the back of his neck and stared out the front window as if he could see Main Street through the grimy glass. "All right, I'll tell you. I'd rather do this somewhere more…" He glanced around the shop. "Pleasant. But here we are. You see, I couldn't explain before I left, because I had to be sure about some things first."

The clock ticked away. Perspiration shone on his temples. He swiped at his forehead and took a deep breath. Now he was the one looking flustered.

"When I enlisted in the army, I left a wife behind."

After observing her reaction, he lowered his eyes.

"We'd been married a few months, and I figured she'd understand I couldn't fight the draft. But it wasn't long until she divorced me. Her letter came just before our first battle. Shocked me—I had no idea. After that, well, maybe before, she took up with somebody else—a neighbor was kind enough to let me know."

He tapped his fingers on the bench. "About a year ago, I found out they got married. But the Army told me they'd never received official notification of our divorce, so I've been trying to sort through all of this."

A dark streak traced his eyes, and his words sounded hollow in the high garage.

"The army's always had a penchant for complicated paperwork, and things can get lost. Even important documents—especially important ones, I'd say. So I had to make sure all the legalities were settled for good before I could move on, even though I've wanted to marry you since New Year's Eve."

"New..." Glenora's thoughts flitted back to that night. So the dance had meant something to him after all.

"Holding you in my arms did it for me. Or maybe it was your wild polka-dot dress." His sheepish grin melted her heart. "Believe me, that night out in your yard after we planted the garden, I wanted to kiss you so much—wanted to tell you everything. It was all I could do..."

"So you've known all along, and I..."

"But I couldn't see my way clear until I knew things were set for sure—that's not how I operate, especially with the most important decision of our lives. I couldn't start out and then have to turn back—wouldn't be fair to you."

She leaned against the counter, thankful the solid old wood held her up. Hank paced over to the far wall and back.

"I spent half of my first college week driving back and forth to Camp Dodge to get this all straightened out. I didn't want the past intruding on our life together. Besides all that, I... well, I hesitated a little, Nora." He stopped pacing a couple of feet away. "Do you mind if I call you that?"

Shaking her head was all she could manage.

"Good. Kissing you the day the war ended... I probably should have controlled myself, or at least asked your forgiveness afterward. But that was when I knew I had to do something. There could never be anyone else for me. Still, I wasn't sure how you'd feel about..."

His eyes glinted. "How you'd feel about a proposal from a divorced man."

Glenora hardly heard him after he said *our life together...*" The phrase floated inside her like a benediction.

"That's why you seemed so distant before you left, but all the time..."

"Yeah, I'm sorry about that."

"I thought you were...upset with me."

He nodded. "I was afraid I'd... I had to be sure about something else, too." A darker ruby deepened Hank's flush. "That enemy sniper gave me another injury, less obvious than this one." He brushed the scar on his face and sought her eyes. "You do want to have children, don't you?'

"Why... yes."

"The doctors at the Vets Hospital in Des Moines checked everything out last week." He wiggled his eyebrows. "And I'm all in good order. I couldn't have saddled you with half a man."

"You must know I would have..."

But Hank held up his hand. "Let me finish." With the other hand, he fished in his pocket and pulled out a sparkling ring. "I spent the other half of my first week searching for this—had no idea diamonds were scarce, with so many troops coming home and getting married."

He motioned her closer, and she obeyed, as though walking in her sleep. He slipped the ring on her finger. Then he smoothed his thumb under her lower lip, sending a shiver down her spine. "I thought I'd catch you at the church, but..."

She could only press her face into the wild thump-thump of Hank's heart. He gave her a gentle push back and looked into her eyes. "So now I can ask you with my whole heart. Will you marry me, Glenora Carson? Have I found the right key?"

She pulled up her head, drew closer into his scent, free of grease today, and let his warm lips drown out her whispered *yes*. When he finally released her, she could barely breathe.

"Now, what was it you started to say earlier?"

"That I'd love you no matter what."

He swept her into his arms and held her for hours, it seemed. "So then. When can you marry me, Miss Carson?"

"Any time. Soon."

"There's no time like the present. How about next Friday, as soon as I can drive up here from my last class?"

She nodded, and he kissed her once again.

117

About the Author

Words have always been comfort food for Gail Kittleson. After instructing expository writing and English as a Second Language, she began writing seriously. Intrigued by the World War II era, Gail creates women's historical fiction from her northern Iowa home and also facilitates writing workshops/retreats.

She and her husband, a retired Army chaplain, enjoy their grandchildren and in winter, Arizona's Mogollon Rim Country. You can count on Gail's heroines to ask honest questions, act with integrity, grow in faith, and face hardships with spunk.

Visit Gail online at: GailKittleson.com